FREAK SHOW

Harem of Freaks Book 1

CRYSTAL ASH

PROLOGUE
THE WOLF MAN

Darkness surrounded me as I came to consciousness. The rumblings of an engine and sway of my surroundings told me I was in a vehicle. Rank smells of long stale bodily fluids of many previous victims filled my nose.

My limbs screamed with fatigue. I tried to move them, only to realize they had been shackled behind my back. I pushed myself up to my knees, only to find my head and shoulders crammed up against the bars of a cage.

Soft whimpers a few feet away sent my ears pricking forward. A heavy sense of dread filled me as my hackles raised.

Dad?

My daughter's frightened voice in my head broke my heart. *No. Not them, too.* They promised they wouldn't touch them. Handing myself over had been for nothing. I should have known better than to trust humans.

Rinna! I answered her. *I'm here, sweetie. Are you hurt?*

Daddy, my head hurts and I can't shift. Roo is sleeping and he won't wake up.

A growl of despair escaped my throat. These monsters captured *both* of my children. What kind of father was I to allow this to happen?

Is he moving at all? I asked her as calmly as I could muster. *Put your ear on his chest for me, sweetie. Can you hear anything?*

I heard a clinking of chains as Rinna shifted around and waited the longest seconds of my life for her answer.

He's breathing, and his heart's thumping, she confirmed.

So my son was still alive. That didn't mean someone wasn't about to get their throat ripped out whenever this truck stopped.

I blinked my eyes and tried to figure out which form I was in. My teeth and ears felt canine, but my senses of smell, sight, and hearing were pathetically dulled and human.

I tried to pull my wolf back and go fully human. But he was stuck. For the first time in my life, I could barely feel the predator within me. Despite having the teeth and ears and fur, it almost felt like the wolf side of me was dead.

Again and again, I attempted to transition to either human or wolf, but both sides wouldn't budge. From what I could feel, I was trapped in some in-between form.

Daddy, what's going to happen to us? Rinna's mental voice cracked with fear that no child should ever experience.

I'm not sure, baby, I confessed. *But I'm going to get us out of here. We'll be with the pack again before you know it.*

The vehicle came to a sudden, screeching halt, sending me slamming up against the bars of my cage. I growled through the pain shooting up my arms, hoping my kids didn't get as hurt as I did.

Voices outside made me bare my teeth. I heard English and then another human language I didn't recognize. When the door rolled up, the light nearly blinded me. But I was ready.

With the most fearsome growl I could summon, I lunged forward and snapped my teeth at the pudgy, skittish humans. Even with my human nose, I could smell the fear and disgust on them.

"FUCK!"

One of them stumbled back, dropping whatever was in his hand.

The other recovered quickly, his eyes dark and cold as he produced a long, electric cattle prod.

My heart sank. I wouldn't be able to touch him with that thing.

"Seems you need to learn some training, dog," he sneered in a heavily accented voice.

He jabbed the weapon toward me and the jolt felt like thousands of tiny knives under my skin. I howled and convulsed uncontrollably, but it was nothing compared to the sound of Rinna whimpering and crying.

"Get your ass in here and shut that other mutt up!" the human on me yelled at his companion.

"Please, they're just children! Do whatever you want to me, but don't hurt them." I forced my mouth to speak the words, but my tongue and throat were not human enough. It came out as garbled grunts and barks.

The human gave me one final look of disgust before he jabbed the weapon into my ribs again.

This time, the darkness swallowed me.

MELODY

My life didn't truly begin until my eighteenth birthday, when I ran away from home.

Every day before that was just another day in trailer trash purgatory. My mother scamming the government for her disability checks, bringing home equally trashy men who disappeared as soon as she got pregnant again.

And me, barely hanging on in high school to help look after all of my younger half-siblings. To be perfectly honest, I don't think any of us shared a father.

My birthday was the weekend after high school graduation. Never in my life had anything been timed so perfectly.

That morning, I woke up early. The house was quiet for once. It would've almost felt peaceful if it weren't for the piles of food containers, beer cans, toys, and everything else imaginable scattered around. I shouldered my backpack that I packed the night before, went out the front door, closed it behind me, and never looked back.

No one was awake to wish me a happy birthday, but that was okay. This was my present to myself.

I didn't have a plan aside from getting as far away from that hell hole as possible. Still, I wasn't some naïve, lost little lamb. Seeing the type of men my mom brought home made me extra vigilant about the people out in the world. I got enough creepy leers and drunken propositions to be constantly on the lookout.

It wasn't all bad, though. I was finally free. No one yelled at me to clean up or make food or get out of the way. I got some strange looks from people at greasy diners and truck stops, but that was to be expected. A skinny girl with ghostly pale skin, dark hair and brown eyes traveling on her own had to be an unusual sight.

I hitchhiked and panhandled for a good part of my trip, but by the time I made it out of my godforsaken state of Alabama, my meager change had run out and I needed to do something different, and fast.

The one positive memory of my childhood years was visiting a traveling carnival with my family. We scraped enough change together to gain entry, play some carnival games and watch a magic show.

It mesmerized me how the magician's cards appeared and disappeared. He turned silk scarves into doves and pulled a live rabbit out of his hat. My siblings and I were all allowed to gently pet the bunny and, to this day, it was the softest thing I ever touched.

The magician even pulled a coin from behind my ear and let me keep it. I never saw anything like it before. It was large and heavy, like a fifty-cent coin, with a border of silver and inlaid with gold. Instead of some politician's head, two crossed daggers were stamped into the metal.

I always carried it with me, knowing one of Mom's boyfriends would steal it if they saw it. As I got older, I watched YouTube videos and practiced the tricks on making it disappear. Just in case I needed it to.

As I walked away from the only home I'd ever known, I clutched that coin in my fist as if to draw strength from my one happy memory.

So I got out my coin and the rough deck of playing cards I bought from a thrift store and parked my ass at a popular rest stop near the freeway.

It was summer time, so it never got too cold at night. If the sightings of wolves didn't scare me, I'd sleep under the stars every night. With the plethora of families going on camping trips to the mountains, I had a steady influx of customers. Kids would shriek with excitement as I curled my fingers over the coin in my palm, then open them slowly to reveal my empty hand.

Parents at first were wary of the skinny, black-haired girl who clearly lived at the rest stop, but they could soon see I was harmless and still had all my mental faculties. I'd been away from home for two weeks at that point and did my best to regularly wash my clothes and body in the rest stop bathroom. My cleaner-than-typical-homeless appearance seemed to put them at ease. I'd entertain the children for a few minutes and their parents gave me enough tips to buy food from the vending machine.

It wasn't easy. And sometimes, when all the travelers left, I got lonely.

But I was free for the first time in my life. I saw beautiful sunsets over the mountains and watched the stars come out. I'd lay down to sleep on the bench, clutching my coin in my fist with a smile on my face. My life was my own, and I was happy. So of course, it couldn't last long.

I woke up early one morning to the sound of crackling static and crunching footsteps. My eyes cracked open and the sight before me jolted me awake. Fear gripped my chest as I sat up abruptly and began scooting away.

"Easy, easy. It's alright."

The uniformed state trooper raised his hands with open palms as his shiny steel-toed boots approached me slowly. I looked like a distorted doll in the mirrored reflection of his sunglasses. My eyes darted to the holstered gun at his hip and then to the squad car parked behind him.

"It's alright, sweetheart," he drawled. "No one's gonna hurt ya."

Did I believe him? Hell no. But while my heart crashed against my ribs, my legs couldn't seem to move.

He removed his sunglasses to peer at me with curious blue eyes. His Tom Selleck mustache twitched as he took me in, studying me.

"You been living out here a while?"

I didn't answer. Clearly, he already knew.

"How old are ya, sweetheart?"

Again, I answered with defiant silence.

"Got any family nearby?" he went on. "I bet your parents are worried about you."

I let out a dark huff of laughter. Yes, Mom would definitely be worried about her live-in maid and babysitter. How else would she be able to watch TV and fuck drunk losers all day?

"I'm eighteen," I said. "My parents don't need to know where I am."

"Ah, she does speak." His mustache twitched with a

hint of a smile. "Well, that makes my job easier. Must've been a rough life to start living at a rest stop, huh?"

"I haven't committed any crimes," I snapped, although I had no idea if that was true. "If you need me to leave here, I'll go."

He crossed his arms, still studying me carefully, as if I was a puzzle he was trying to decipher.

"What're your plans for the winter?" he asked. "What are you going to do about shelter?"

I shrugged. "Head down to Florida, maybe. I haven't thought that far ahead yet."

"Obviously," he scoffed.

I bristled with annoyance. When was this cop going to stop wasting my time?

"Look, I'll make a deal with ya," he said. "I'll buy you some breakfast and give you a ride over to the next town. They have good services in place for the homeless."

My stomach chose that moment to betray me and let out an echoing growl. After living off vending machine food for a week, a real cooked meal sounded absolutely heavenly. Some hash browns, pancakes, fresh fruit, maybe even an omelet with some bacon. And a cup of fresh, piping hot coffee. And doughnuts.

The cop's smile grew wider as he watched my food fantasies dance in my head. That small gesture brought me back to reality. If I knew anything, it was that men never offered anything unless they wanted something in return.

"And what do you expect to get out of this?" I asked, trying to keep a tough edge to my voice.

He shook his head. "Just the peace of mind of knowing a young lady who reminds me of my daughter will be safe."

The curiosity in his gaze softened and for the first

time, I saw warmth and protectiveness that I never saw growing up. The parental affection that I read about in books and heard rumors of, but never experienced for myself. I swore it was a myth, some kind of fairy tale.

"What's your name, sweetheart?" he asked gently.

I hesitated, but decided to answer truthfully.

"Melody."

"Nice to meet you, Melody. I'm Rick."

Rick began to turn back toward the parking lot, but kept his eyes focused on me.

"The car is warm if you want to follow me. It'll be a short ride into town. The sooner we go, the sooner we can get food in your belly and a proper bed for you to sleep on. How does that sound, Melody?"

"You can call me Mel," I said in a small voice, slowly lowering my feet from the bench to the ground.

Rick smiled affectionately. "Alright then, Mel. We'll go whenever you're ready."

He turned and began walking back to his squad car, talking in some police code into the radio clipped to his shirt.

I put both feet on the floor and considered running into the woods. He was an older guy and probably wouldn't be able to catch me. But then where would I go? He probably checked out this rest stop regularly. And while small towns dotted this stretch of highway into the mountains, I had no map or phone. I could be lost for days before finding food or safe water to drink.

It dawned on me that this cop knew that. He knew I could run off, and he'd never catch me. He never came closer than ten feet to me. He'd never even have the opportunity to put handcuffs on me if he really wanted to force me anywhere.

He gave me space, and from that I realized he was giving me a choice. Death or doughnuts? It wasn't a hard decision to make.

So I stood from my bench and touched the coin in my pocket. I picked up my bag and blanket, and hesitantly shuffled toward the police officer, patiently waiting in his car. He reached across to open the passenger door for me and I sank into the seat like a warm cocoon.

We drove in relative silence, which I was grateful for. I didn't want to answer questions.

"What kinda breakfast you in the mood for, Mel?" he asked.

"Um, anything." My stomach agreed.

"Figured you wouldn't be picky," he chuckled.

The dense forest began clearing out as we passed a sign that said "Welcome to Drowningville!"

Really? I thought. I couldn't think of a town name that sounded any less welcoming.

We stopped at a drive-thru and I inhaled my breakfast the moment Rick passed the paper bag to me.

"Slow down, Mel. You'll get sick," he warned.

Yeah, that wasn't happening. It smelled too good and tasted like greasy, piping-hot heaven.

As we drove through town and I sat back to digest my food, I noticed that Drowningville looked like a carbon copy of my hometown, Waterford. Potholes in the streets, run-down trailer parks, and graffiti on buildings galore. A tightening in my chest gripped me and I started to regret leaving my rest stop sanctuary. What was the point of returning to civilization if I was just going back to fighting for survival in another shithole town all over again?

"Here we are," Rick said.

We pulled up in front of a large, rundown house, and my heart sank. How many people just like my mother and her boyfriends would be in there?

"Now listen, Mel," Rick said, turning to me. "You're so young. You still have a long, full life ahead of you. If you take advantage of their resources and accept help, you'll be just fine."

But I barely paid attention to him. My eyes drifted over his shoulder to look at the sign on the fence across the street.

It said, "TRAVELING CARNIVAL IN TOWN FOR ONE WEEK ONLY!"

MELODY

"So what special talents do you have?" Mr. Fisher, the carnival manager, leered at me, not bothering to hide that he was ogling at my breasts. "What unique abilities can you add to my carnival?"

I cleared my throat and pulled my tank top up as best I could. I couldn't help the fact that it was a typical Mississippi summer, hot and muggy as the devil's armpit, nor that my top was tiny and threadbare. I had it since sophomore year and never could afford to buy more clothes since then. This stuffy, worn-down trailer with no fan or air conditioning definitely didn't help.

Still, I plastered what I hoped was a friendly smile on my face and pulled out my lucky coin.

"I can do simple magic tricks." I demonstrated by closing my fist around the coin and slowly opening my fingers to show him my empty hand. "And I'm a fast learner, so I'd be happy to shadow senior magicians and pick up more tricks by watching them."

"Ah, you have good enthusiasm dear, but you see," he

leaned across the cheap plywood desk, shamelessly never removing his eyes from my chest, "magicians will never reveal their tricks. A true magician is self-taught. I'm proud to say that everyone in my carnival put in the work themselves without shadowing anyone. And I prefer to keep it that way." He leaned back, lacing his fingers together on his massive belly. "Anything else?"

I huffed in annoyance, feeling my cheeks grow warm. "Well, I can read tarot cards, too. I can look into a crystal ball and pretend I see the future. Basically, I can put on a great act."

He didn't seem convinced. My heart sank as he pursed his lips in thought while tapping a pencil on his desk.

"I already have talented people in those jobs, Miss. People that have been perfecting their acts for years. Why should I just take in a pretty girl off the street?"

"I can bring something new to the table," I insisted. "Seriously, I can improvise on the fly and put my own spin on things. I promise I can bring in lots of money for you."

He gave a smile that I couldn't read. It looked like an odd mixture of patronizing, predatory, and pitying.

"Do you *really* want to work at a carnival?" he asked.

"Yes!" I answered without hesitation.

He raised one thick, bushy eyebrow in amusement. "Why?"

I thought for a moment, wondering how much of my shitty life I should tell him. Distantly, I remembered a class in school about how to act during a job interview. The teacher said not to divulge overly personal information or something like that. I couldn't remember, but I was pretty sure I was about to break that rule.

"Because the carnival was the only glimpse of happiness during my childhood," I admitted. "The music, the games, the shows. It devastated me when all the fun and mystery and wonder came to an end. I didn't understand that it would be temporary. I wanted to live there and be happy forever."

I sat back, deflated and already sure that I bombed this interview. So why stop there? "And I want to give the attendees a reason to laugh and smile, just in case they came from the same kind of crappy life as me."

Mr. Fisher sighed and ran a hand through his thinning hair. "Look kid, I can tell you're on hard times right now and need a job. But working the carnival isn't an easy job. Every one of my performers here has very specialized skills. It takes years and years of practice to perfect these skills. You don't just wake up one day and realize you can juggle or ride a unicycle, you know?"

I nodded, lowering my eyes to my lap.

"Furthermore, it's a temporary job," he continued. "We travel for a while during summer and early fall and that's it, really. A kid like you needs stability. Something to build a foundation on so you can have a good life, you know?"

I nodded my agreement while picking at the dirt under my fingernails, wondering when he'd finish so I could leave.

"A pretty little thing like you wouldn't fit in with this freak show anyway," he laughed. "You oughta get an education, a regular job and settle down with a nice guy working in finance or some shit. Have his babies and a house with a white picket fence and all that."

I couldn't help but snort out a laugh at that. The notion of *me*, trailer park trash to a T, raising kids in the suburbs with some bland, boring guy couldn't be more ridiculous. All I wanted to do was not end up pregnant by some deadbeat drunk like my mom and older sister.

So far, I was doing pretty well for myself in that regard and had no intention of stopping. Aside from me, no woman in my immediate family made it to eighteen without getting knocked up.

"That's kind of you, sir, but I don't think that's in the cards for me," I said, holding back my giggles.

He looked taken aback. "Why the hell not? You're young and beautiful with your life ahead of you!"

"Sir, if you're not going to give me a chance at the carnival," I said, rising to unstick my sweaty thighs from my folding chair. "Then I'm heading to the strip club up the street because that's my best option right now."

His pupils dilated, and I shuddered to know what he was picturing in his mind.

"You'd make a hell of a lot more money there," he pointed out.

"Yeah, maybe," I agreed. "But I wouldn't enjoy it as much. Who knows?" I chuckled, moving toward the door. "If I learn some special moves as a stripper, I might ask you again for a job as a contortionist next year." My eyes bore into his. "That's how much I love the carnival. I don't care how much it pays." I turned toward the flimsy plywood door of the trailer. "Thanks a lot for your time, Mr. Fisher."

My hand just turned the knob when he called out, "Melody, wait."

I paused, turning back toward him. "Yes?"

He huffed out a heavy breath before speaking. "If you're willing to be a team player, and work various menial jobs behind the scenes, I might be able to find a position for you."

"Really?" I faced him directly, my eyes daring to widen with hope.

"You won't be part of any acts, at least not the main part," he said. "But if you're willing to smile and dress a little sexy, I can make you a stage assistant. On slow nights maybe you can pour drinks at the booze tent, whatever we can find for you."

I ran forward and wrapped my arms around the large, sweaty man's neck in a bear hug. He reeled back, startled, before tentatively patting my back with his meaty hands.

"Oh, thank you so much, Mr. Fisher!" I squealed. "This is all I wanted, just a chance to show what I can do!"

"I want to reiterate that it's not easy work," he warned when I untangled myself from him. He tried to look stern, but I could see the smile playing at his lips and his face flushed a deep red. "You'll probably be driven harder than the performers. You're starting at the bottom of the ladder essentially, and if you want to climb up, expect to do it kicking and clawing and maybe throwing a few elbows."

"Oh, I'm no stranger to hard work," I said, bobbing my head in a nod. "Honestly, I'm dying to get started! When do you want me to come in?"

He flashed a toothy grin at me. "How about tonight?"

⚜ 3 ⚜

MELODY

I turned over rocks with my worn-out shoes as I waited outside the trailer for Mr. Fisher. After my interview, he told me to come back in four hours and meet him here. He'd "find a place to fit me in," as he put it.

I brought up my concern about proper attire or equipment I'd need. All I had were the spare change of clothes in my backpack, my lucky coin, and a deck of worn-out playing cards. He told me not to worry, that whatever position I had would come with a uniform and they'd tailor it to my size.

Another minute passed, and I sighed, growing more anxious by the minute. Should I try knocking on the door again? Or maybe a better question was, should I even be here?

Most eighteen-year-olds were applying to colleges, working part-time jobs in fast food and retail. Those kids were setting the tracks down for their life plans. But I imagined most of those kids didn't have to worry about their mom's endless string of boyfriends wandering drunkenly into their bedroom at night. The same bedroom I shared with my younger siblings, who cried in absolute terror at the huge, grunting men stumbling around our trailer at all hours of the night.

No, I didn't dream of a college experience, joining a sorority, or even having a boyfriend. The only thing that ever put a smile on my face was the carnival, so that was the only dream I chased.

With a deep breath, I raised my first to rap on the door again just as it swung open.

"Ah, Melody! Right on time," Mr. Fisher greeted with his signature toothy grin. "Come in, come in."

Yes, I had been on time. He made me wait an additional fifteen minutes.

I followed him into the dimly lit trailer and the smell of stale cigarettes and booze assaulted my nostrils. Growing up how I did, I got used to that smell, but that brief week in the fresh mountain air had spoiled me. I missed my temporary rest-stop home in that moment but remembered I wanted this job, and this life.

A busty middle-aged woman with thick blonde hair sat in a creaky, rolling office chair. Wearing nothing but stockings with a garter belt, underwear, and a bra that just barely contained her massive breasts, she reminded me of a classier version of my mother. The woman inspected me with dark, hooded eyes through the smoke clouds she blew.

"Damn, Peter," she said in a crackling smoker's voice. "I knew you liked 'em young, but this is a new leap even for you."

"I'm eighteen," I piped up. "I do have a valid ID."

The woman let out a laugh that sounded like crumbling paper.

"We ain't worried about your ID, sweetheart," she croaked. "But I ain't convinced your young eyes won't fall out your damn head when you see what goes on 'round here."

"I might be young, but I've seen plenty of things that no girl my age should see," I shot back, crossing my arms. "Trust me, I ain't no damn princess."

My defensiveness brought out my own redneck twang that I fought hard to keep at bay. Normally, I hated sounding like white trash, but with this woman, it might actually give me some credit.

She took a hard drag on her cigarette and smirked. "Ever seen two drunk dwarves fuckin' behind the tents?"

Heat rose in my cheeks, but I kept my expression bitchy. "Naw. Seen two drunk-ass, coked out junkies fuck a hole through the carpet, though."

That got a thunderous, booming laugh from her and a nervous giggle and blush from Mr. Fisher. Something told me while he held the manager title, this woman was the one who really ran the show.

"You just might be alright, girly." She flashed a yellowed, gap-toothed grin that seemed approving. "What's your name?"

"Melody. I go by Mel."

"Nah-uh." She flicked an orange plastic lighter and lit another cigarette. "You'll be introduced as Melody. It's sexy like a stripper name. The crowd'll love it."

"Uh." I started to protest, but held my tongue. Hopefully she didn't mean I would *actually* be stripping. "Okay. So this means you're hiring me, Mrs., uh?"

"Madame," she corrected me with a wink. "Madame Tetons." She leaned forward and shimmied her shoulders back and forth, making her *tetons* sway hypnotically behind her tiny bra. A guffaw of laughter was her reaction to my reddening face, which also burned uncomfortably. Maybe I was a little unaccustomed to carnival life, but that didn't mean I still couldn't fit in.

"And sure, honey. You're hired for as long as your pretty face can handle being around this freak show." Madame Tetons grinned. "You'll get cash at the end of the night. Makes no difference to me whether or not you're here the next day."

"I'll keep coming back to work," I insisted. "Really, I'm responsible. I wouldn't just walk away from a job like that."

"We'll see, sugar," she chuckled, stubbing out her cigarette in a glass ashtray overflowing with butts. "Let's get ya fixed up then."

She stood abruptly and headed for the trailer door, shoving it open so hard it bounced off the outside wall. I looked over at Mr. Fisher who'd remained nearly silent during this whole meeting. He shrugged and motioned for me to follow Madame Tetons out the door.

"I got a show to run, sweet cheeks! You comin' or not?" she hollered from outside.

I hurriedly followed her fast, but slightly wobbly gait. Her walk reminded me of Jack Sparrow. She led me to a large circus tent and slapped back the flap, much like she did to the trailer door. I followed her in to find a group of women in various states of undress. Like Madame Tetons, some wore stockings and garter belts. Others wore corsets, tutus, and impossibly high heels.

Oversized trunks and suitcases made for temporary chairs and sofas. A pair of women sat on an antique-looking wooden trunk sharing a bottle of liquor as they giggled with their heads bowed. Portable closets on rusty wheels were bursting with various costumey clothing items. A few vanities and full-length mirrors completed the tent furnishings.

"Cherry!" Madame Tetons barked at a young woman with flaming box-dyed red hair. "This is Melody. Find her something to wear. She's Syko's dartboard tonight."

While Cherry inspected me from head to toe as if appraising me, I turned to Madame Tetons, who was already quickly exiting the tent.

"Wait!" I called after her, sticking my head out of the tent. "What does that mean, I'm a *dartboard?*"

"What's it sound like?" she cackled as she Jack Sparrowed away.

"Don't worry, hun," Cherry drawled from behind me. "Syk's a good shot. Best knife thrower on this side of the Mississippi. He won't cut ya unless he's hittin' the bottle too hard." I turned back to face her, my face white as a ghost, to find her showing me a small scar on the side of her hip. "He gave me a good nick when I dartboarded for him last summer. He was so fuckin' hammered, he don't even remember doing the show." She ran her tongue across her teeth and grinned. "He kissed it all better, though." Her expression turned venomous as she lifted her chin and gave me her best bitch stare. "And if you even look at him too long, I'll cut yer damn neck myself."

I raised my hands in a *yeah, whatever* motion. Alcoholic men were a dime a dozen, and I'd be happy to never see one again.

"Look, I just wanna get through the night in one piece so I can get my cash at the end," I told her.

Cherry nodded as if she approved of that answer and led me away from the tent flap to a rolling wardrobe stuffed with clothes and accessories. I squared my shoulders and took deep breaths as I followed her. Having knives thrown at me wasn't my idea of a good time, but if this Syko guy was that good, hopefully I'd come out injury-free and be assigned a different job tomorrow night.

"What's yer tit size?" Cherry asked brusquely as she looked at me up and down.

"Um, 34B," I mumbled, knowing I was blushing. Everyone else here seemed to at least have a C cup, if not DD. I tried not to stare, but they all filled out their corsets and push-up bras perfectly. I never filled out to that curvaceous, well-fed body type that seemed to send men's tongues wagging. My mom ate and drank her welfare check the moment she got it, and the bulk of whatever little we had left went to my siblings.

Not that I *wanted* a bunch of idiot redneck men chasing after me, but I knew lots of eyes would be on me tonight. I wanted to make a good impression.

Cherry rifled through the rack of clothing as I stood there, pausing only to look at me briefly before rifling some more.

"Try this on," she said, picking out a black corset that looked entirely too small, even for my slender frame.

Still, I turned toward the nearest full-length mirror and removed my shirt and bra so she could help me into it. After a few moments of lacing and sucking in, I regretted that decision.

"It doesn't fit," I wheezed as Cherry continued tugging on the stings.

"Yeah, it does. You just need to suck it in more."

"I can't... anymore."

She finally stopped tugging as I struggled to breathe, not only with how tight she laced it but now that my breasts were shoved up into my face.

"It's a new one so you'll break it in if you stick around." She gave me a not-so-subtle side eye as she went back to rummaging through clothes.

After another twenty minutes or so, the leather corset did seem to give more room for my lungs to expand. In that time, Cherry also found me stockings, shoes, sheer gloves, a distressed tulle skirt, an elaborate choker necklace that brought even more attention to my chest and at her insistence, a goddamn top hat.

"Come on. Make up next," she said, dragging me to a nearby vanity and plopping me down.

I cringed at the amount of purple and glitter she smeared on my lips and eyelids, feeling certain that she was doing me in clown makeup. Along with my ridiculous outfit, people would be eager to throw pies at me after the knives.

Remember, you wanted this, I told myself. *Maybe not this job tonight, but this life. You want to entertain and bring smiles. This is worlds better than what you ran from. And tonight, the cash you earn is going to be all yours. No one's gonna steal it for booze.*

"There," Cherry said, stepping back to look at me. "Take a look but I ain't changing shit."

Bracing myself, I turned to the mirror and my purple lips fell open at what I saw.

I looked hot. Like, *damn* hot.

Yes, it was a ton of makeup and the colors were bright and dramatic, but it was perfect for being onstage at a carnival. My eyebrows were full and arched seductively. The false eyelashes fluttered like butterfly wings. And the pink apples of my cheeks glittered when I smiled.

"Uh, wow. Thanks, Cherry," I said sincerely. "It looks good. You're really talented."

She shrugged nonchalantly, but I could tell the compliment pleased her.

"Use the bobby pins to keep the hat on your head. Don't wanna lose it when you go upside down."

"Upside down?" I blinked at her.

"Damn girl," she giggled. "You really have no idea what you're in for."

❦ 4 ❧

MELODY

"**C**ome on, let's head to Syko's tent." Cherry grabbed my wrist and pulled me along while I teetered on my sky-high heels. "It ain't rocket science, but you'll wanna rehearse the act. 'Specially since you have no idea what the fuck you're getting into."

"Uh, yeah. Makes sense." I dutifully followed her out of the tent and into the late afternoon heat.

Looking around, I realized the carnival was in full swing right at that moment. The distant sounds of laughter and music filled my senses. I could even smell the deep fried food and funnel cake. In the distance, the Ferris wheel turned slowly like the orbit of a distant planet.

Cherry and I walked through a cluster of tents and trailers on one side of the carnival, a good hundred feet or so from where families played games and ate snow cones. A string of brightly colored flags tied to two trees separated the trailers and tents from the main carnival area. This had to be where all the staff and performers stayed out of the public eye when off duty.

We didn't walk far, but my skin was already covered in a thin sheen of sweat and my stiletto heels sank into the mud. I could only pray that my caked-on makeup wouldn't start sliding off my face. Cicadas sang their song, and the air was thick with moisture each time I took a breath. Fuck, I hated the south in the summer.

Cherry approached one of the large pavilions and slapped open the flap, not bothering to hold it for me as I followed her in.

"I gotcher dartboard, baby." Her voice suddenly took on a higher pitch as she walked up to a man wearing a wifebeater tank top and pinstriped pants, which I assumed was the lower half of his uniform.

"Yeah? Let's see who's savin' my show," he drawled, taking a gratuitous grab of her ass as she wrapped her arms around his neck. But his eyes remained on me and they sent a shiver along my spine despite the sweltering heat.

This guy instantly gave me the creeps. He looked to be in his late forties, with skinny arms and a soft belly. Tufts of salt and pepper chest hair poked out from the neck of his wife-beater. His flushed face with broken blood vessels confirmed my dread that this guy was indeed an alcoholic.

And he was going to be throwing knives at me.

"Damn, she's a young one." His eyes crawled over me like inspecting a piece of meat. "What's yer name, sweetheart?"

"Melody," I answered with a smile in an attempt to hide my discomfort.

"Well, keep smilin' like that, miss Melody, and we're gonna get along just fine," he grinned, revealing yellow teeth. "I'm Syko. Drink?" He waved a hand toward a rolling cart with various bottles of liquor.

"No thanks," I said, my smile tightening.

"You sure? It'll calm your nerves." He winked. "Not that you got anythin' to be nervous about."

"I'm good, thanks. And I'm not that nervous, mainly just excited to put on a good show!" I squeaked out, my cheeks already hurting from my smile.

"I like your spirit, Melody." His tone and creepy stare indicated he liked my tits in this corset a lot more. "Maybe you could teach ol' Stilts a thing or two about a positive attitude. Eh, Stilts?"

Laughing, Syko turned to a man I hadn't even noticed in the tent. He appeared to be taking a nap on the floor, with his head and upper back propped up against a large backpack and a tattered blanket thrown over his legs.

Damn, I thought. If I wanted anyone to appreciate my tits in this outfit, it would be him. A sun-kissed tan and lean muscle covered his chest and arms. His dark brown hair was tousled as if he ran his fingers through it, his slightly pursed lips looked so kissable as he slept. A shadow of stubble peppered coated his angular jaw. If he heard Syko's comment, he gave no indication.

The creepy man marched over and nudged him with his foot, clearly displeased at being ignored.

Stilts cocked open one forest green eye and grunted out his annoyance.

"The fuck you want, Syk?" he grumbled, his voice vibrating with a low, sexy thunder.

"We have a new girl for the dartboard," Syko answered, gesturing toward me.

The sleepy green eye scanned the room but barely paused on me. "Is it show time?"

"No, I just thought we'd--"

"Don't fuckin' wake me up until it's show time or I'll break your fuckin' jaw." Stilts grabbed a beanie and pulled it down over his head and eyes, effectively ending the conversation.

I stifled a giggle. Like the pompous ass he was, Syko tried to show me off like a new prized possession, and this guy didn't give an iota of a fuck. I liked that he didn't join in appraising my body like at a meat market, although I wouldn't mind if he noticed me a little more.

"Fuck this guy." Syko waved at him dismissively. "Let's rehearse the act just me and you, sweetheart."

The sound of a throat clearing reminded both of us that Cherry was still in the tent. Syko gave her a dismissive wave too.

"Go on, girlie. I'm sure you got somewhere to be."

Her face fell and I couldn't help but feel bad for her, no matter how much of a creepy scumbag Syko was.

"I'll see ya later, right, baby?" she asked hopefully.

"Yeah, yeah. At the booze tent when the show's over. Now getcher ass out. I got work to do."

She shot me a death glare before slapping the tent flap and storming outside. My heart sank at seeing her go. I had a feeling I wouldn't make many friends in this business, but that was okay. I'd made it to eighteen years without any friends and learned to live with it.

"Come on, darlin'." Syko grabbed my hand and yanked me so hard, I nearly toppled over in my heels.

He dragged me out the back door of the tent and to a clearing where other carnival performers seemed to be practicing their acts. Two people chatted casually while juggling bowling pins and riding unicycles. A group of acrobats practiced a beautiful, flowing routine on a set of tables and makeshift trapeze hung between two branches of a tree. I covered my mouth to hold in my scream when a man flawlessly dropped a dagger down his throat and spun the handle around.

"Here we are, darlin'," Syko cooed at me. Pet names were common in the south but damn, I wished he'd stop.

My eyes fell upon what was obviously a human-sized dartboard. A round piece of wood just slightly taller than me, with slender black and white triangles pointing toward a red bull's eye in the center. Nicks, dents, and chipped paint showed just how often this board had been used. There didn't seem to be any blood on it, thankfully.

"First part of the act," Syko explained, standing too close to me, "is you just standing pretty there in front of the board while I throw. Think you can handle that?"

"Sounds easy enough." I forced a smile.

He delivered an unexpected slap to my ass, which made me jump with a small shriek.

"Then git on over there so I can warm up, darlin'." He pulled a silver flask from his pants pocket and took a long pull while I hurried away, trying to not sink into any muddy spots with my heels.

Grateful to be away from him, yet increasingly dreading the idea of this drunken lowlife throwing knives at me, I forced myself to stand in front of the dartboard. The bulls-eye met the center of my back, while the top of my head just barely grazed the top edge of the board. Only my stupid top hat gave me any extra height.

"Strike a pose and smile, honey." Syko produced a beautiful lacquered case and opened it, revealing four eight-inch-long stainless steel blades polished to a high shine.

Fuck! He was practicing with *real* knives? In my naivete, I'd assumed he'd use dull or dummy knives at least.

But still I flashed a smile, placed my hands at my waist, and cocked my hip to the side. My heart thrummed with lightning speed despite the stillness in my limbs.

Syko made a low, throaty sound that I tried to ignore. "That's perfect, babe. Now don't move a muscle."

I was so consumed by fear and anxiety, I couldn't have moved if I tried.

He turned and walked about 25 feet away from me, about the length of a stage. His next movement was so fast and fluid, I didn't realize he threw the knife until I heard the *thunk* of that steel blade embed into the wood just above my arm.

For a moment, the creepy drunk disappeared and was replaced by a lithe, dancing figure moving with precision. Watching him was mesmerizing. His knife throws were strong and sure, but they flowed seamlessly with his spinning, graceful movements.

By the time all four blades were embedded deep in the wood, my fear—of being stabbed at least—had completely disappeared. I brought my hands together to clap as Syko took a graceful bow.

"That was amazing!" I breathed.

"Thank ya kindly, darlin'." He shot me a saccharine smile. "But you ain't seen nothin' yet."

My heart rate picked up as he came over, standing very close to me again as he removed his blades from the wood and set them in the grass.

"This next part's a doozy," he said, sneaking glances

down to my chest. "But you gotta remember to trust me, alright?"

I nodded as fear gripped my stomach in knots again. Why couldn't I just *say* I didn't feel right about this?

"See that little peg there?" He leaned down, brushing the side of my leg as he pointed out a dowel about eight inches long sticking out from the board. "Step on it for me."

I did as he instructed and he pointed out the other one next to my other foot. For balance, I spread my arms wide and gripped the edges of the board, teetering in my ridiculous heels on two flimsy pegs of wood.

"You got the right idea there." Syko looked all too pleased as he pulled strips of silk from his pockets. They looked like those scarves pulled out of hats and sleeves during magic tricks, but I immediately knew that wasn't his intention here.

He knelt at my feet and swiftly tied one scarf around my ankle and then the other. I was secured to the board by him tying through two holes I didn't notice before. When he stood, he was so close that his chest brushed against mine, his foul breath coming out with lusty grunts. I turned my head and closed my eyes, praying for this practice run to be over soon.

"Trust me," he repeated, taking hold of one of my wrists and laying it flat against the board somewhere above my head. He threaded one of the scarves through the holes there, binding my wrist down tight and then the other.

I was tied to the circular dartboard, arms and legs outstretched like the *Vitruvian Man*. Syko stepped back and to the side as if to admire his handiwork.

"How long do I have to stay like this?" I asked, panic creeping into my voice. I couldn't escape now even if I wanted to. Fuck, why didn't I just speak up?

"Not long, honey. Don't worry." He picked up his knives and flashed me that predatory smile as he leaned one hand on the board, in no apparent hurry. "Just one practice run and I'll go slow." He leaned his weight into his hand and I felt my whole body tilt to the side. "Hope you don't get motion sickness."

He pressed down hard, and suddenly the world was spinning.

No, *I* was spinning.

My stomach churned, but not from the feeling of going up, down, and around again. About twenty-five feet away, Syko stood ready with his knives.

Oh, God! Oh God, please! There's no way!

I watched his figure spin, dance, and take aim, all while spinning around and around. My eyes squeezed shut. The fear of everything, plus the dizziness and disorientation from spinning, was too much.

Thunk, thunk, thunk!

I felt the breeze and vibration from the blades sinking into the wood all around me, but no pain.

Thunk! That was four. The last one.

I cracked my eyes open to see Syko jogging toward me, spinning much slower now.

"See, that wasn't so bad!" He was cheerful as he spun me upright and untied my wrists and ankles. My whole world still spun, and I held onto the board for support, my other hand pressed to my racing heart.

"Hey, listen." He grabbed my face roughly and jerked

my chin up to look at him. His scowl down at me revealed at least two rotting teeth.

"You can't do that shutting your eyes and looking away shit when we're up on stage, you got it?" he growled. "Keep your eyes open. Keep looking at the crowd. And fucking smile. You gotta at least pretend you're having a good time. Otherwise we get a lower turnout and we all get paid less. You got that?"

I nodded, still trying to fight off the dizziness, but flashed him a smile just to show that I understood.

"Got it!" I chirped cheerfully.

He looked pleased again, finally letting go of my face. "Good." My jaw throbbed from where he grabbed me and I wondered if I'd have to reapply makeup.

"Show starts in an hour," he said, looking out at the sun setting behind the trees. "Families'll take their damn brats home and once night falls, the freaks'll come out to play."

He slapped my ass again, making me jump, but also too shocked to protest.

"Go on and get touched up, baby," he grinned, heading off for his own tent. "Almost showtime."

MELODY

I found my way back to the dressing tent and reapplied my makeup. After Syko kicked her out of the tent, Cherry seemed dead set on avoiding me. With a sigh, I shut my eyes and quickly spritzed my face with the setting spray. Would it do any good to explain I didn't *want* his creepy attention? Probably not.

Reaching into my backpack stuffed with my street clothes, I felt around until my lucky coin pressed into my palm and inserted it down the front of my corset. Who knew if it was worth anything of real value, but it was the only sentimental object I owned. And right then, I needed any luck I could squeeze out of it.

"Hey, new girl," Cherry snapped from across the tent. Apparently, she had forgotten my name already. "Show time. We gather at the side of the stage."

I hurried over, trying to keep from toppling in my heels. "When do I go on? I don't know when my act is."

"You go on second," she told me flatly, looking straight ahead with her arms crossed. "First the ringmaster announces, then it's Stilts, then you guys. Syk will call you out when it's your time."

"Thanks," I said sincerely.

She merely grunted, and I withered a little. Still, I followed her to the main stage at the far end of the carnival. The setting sun finally cooled off the temperatures a bit, though not by much. In the main carnival area across the trailers, tents, and gates separating us, voices chattered with excitement.

Already the feeling was different from earlier in the day. Rather than families playing games and eating corn dogs with their children, the evening patrons were almost entirely adults. They talked excitedly, but in low whispers as if this was some secret adventure.

Cherry and I joined the throng of performers and assistants gathered around the side and back of the main stage. I recognized a few of the acrobats and the dagger swallower who practiced earlier. Surely those were the later acts. They'd be far more interesting to watch than a girl get knives thrown at her.

A sudden, loud drumbeat sent my heart feeling like it would crash out of my chest. Claps and cheers erupted from the crowd, sending my pulse into overdrive. It just registered to me right then that I would be getting on stage, performing for an audience. Sure, I'd just be standing around and smiling but that thought did nothing to calm my nerves.

"'Scuse me, ladies!"

A middle-aged man in a top hat just slightly taller than mine jumped down his trailer's steps, straightened the lapels of his red tailcoat, and jogged past us up to the stage on shiny black riding boots.

He strode confidently to the center and the crowd went wild with cheers.

"Ladies and gentlemen, boys and girls!" he bellowed. "Welcome to the opening night of The Voodoo Trail traveling carnival! Prepare to watch in wonder as our performers stun and amaze you! For our entire five-night stay here in Drowningville, each show will be more jaw-dropping, chill-inducing, and death-defying than the last!"

He paused and surveyed the crowd with a wide grin as they cheered and applauded.

"Yes, indeed. We're just getting started folks! We know you'll enjoy yourselves tonight, so make sure you keep coming back until our final night." He dropped his voice and leaned forward, looking across every face with an eerie smile. The crowd hushed to a low murmur, eager to hear what he would say.

"On our last night, we'll reveal a most terrifying, exhilarating, awe-inducing, freak of nature." He removed his top hat and dramatically placed it over his heart. "If you believe in God, my good people, you will *not* want to miss this exhibition. For I can prove to you we have in our possession a true demon from the depths of Hell."

That sent the crowd into a tizzy. It was the South. Of course, God was a huge part of everyone's lives.

"And this is no ordinary demon!" the ringmaster continued, feeding off the crowd's amped up curiosity. "This is one of the most, no, *the* most vile creature I've ever set eyes on! Imagine a beast who stands upright like a man, but with razor-sharp teeth, claws like a bear, glowing yellow eyes, and covered from head to toe in hideous, mangy fur!"

"Show us now!"

"Prove it!"

"Yeah, right! Let's see it!"

The audience began shouting their demands, becoming even more eager as they hung onto his every word. In contrast, all the performers surrounding me looked completely bored. Cherry even yawned.

The ringmaster held up an index finger and waved it from side to side, shaking his head at the same time.

"Now, I know some of you may be thinking this is a hoax or that our captured beast is merely a very hairy man, but I assure you that's not the case! However," he curled his finger back into his fist and the crowd went silent again. "Friday night, you will all see for yourselves, the *Wolf Man*," he said, barely above a whisper.

"But tonight!" he raised his voice again and twirled around theatrically while placing his top hat back on his head. "We have an amazing show to whet your appetites, folks! Bring out the one, the only, Stilts, the acrobatic stilt walker!"

The drums picked up again as he exited the stage in a flourish. Running past me and the rest of the girls, he dashed back to his trailer, where I could only assume his booze, drugs, or prostitute were waiting. Maybe all of the above.

Gasps and cries took my attention back to the stage, and my jaw dropped.

It was the sleeping guy from Syko's tent. He was well over ten feet tall on his stilts and wore an intricate carnival mask, but those forest green eyes pierced me for half a fleeting second. And his act was *amazing*.

He wore long, brightly colored pants for the illusion that he really was freakishly tall. And he moved so fluidly that if it weren't for the stumps of wood at the bottom of his pants, anyone watching could easily believe those were his actual legs. He did handstands, back flips, and tons of gravity-defying moves that looked like a mixture of gymnastics and break dancing. The crowd went wild, forgetting all about the ringmaster's teasing about some freakish Wolf Man, and became just as entranced and mesmerized in Stilts' performance as I was.

The whole time I watched with my mouth hanging open, and briefly wondered why such an amazing act was the opener, and why he didn't have a better stage name than Stilts.

"That was amazing!" I cried, joining in the applause when he finished with a deep bow and headed off the opposite side of the stage from us.

"Yeah, he's good," Cherry agreed. "And a damn fine thing to look at. Too bad he's an asshole." She had produced a small silver flask from somewhere and swayed on her feet a little. Apparently, booze made her a tad friendlier, too.

"Why do you say that?" I asked, not wanting to miss the opportunity to know before she remembered she hated me.

"Psh. You saw how he was in the tent." She waved her hand and rolled her eyes. "He's always like that. To everybody. Just a rude-ass motherfucker."

Yeah, but can you blame him for being rude to a gross pervert like Syko?

I didn't say that out loud.

The crowd started up again as two assistants moved Syko's huge dartboard onto the stage. My stomach jumped into my throat again as I remembered what I would have to do.

The man himself stepped up, wearing a full pinstriped suit with a bowler hat.

"Welcome! Welcome, everyone!" he greeted the crowd jovially while casually flipping a dagger in each hand. "Are you all ready for a hell of a show tonight?"

The crowd answered back with a raucous cheer.

"Mm, he's so charismatic." Cherry was already swooning. I just looked at her like she sprouted an extra head. What on *earth* did she see in that guy?

"Let me tell ya, folks! I am one hell of a knife thrower, but I can't entertain y'all on my own," he said. I swallowed, but the dry lump in my throat would not disappear. "Allow me to introduce you to my beautiful, radiant assistant, Melody!"

He turned and beckoned me with a finger, that grin on his face boisterous and fun to the crowd, but creepy and predatory to me.

Still, I walked out under the bright stage lights on what I hoped were long, confident strides. I plastered a smile on my face and waved to the crowd. Hundreds of eyes stared back at me, cheering and hollering. The men were loudest, their tongues practically wagging at my tits, nearly bursting from my corset.

Syko took my hand and had me do a little twirl, much to the audience's appreciation. My face burned. I would have looked like a tomato if my makeup wasn't so caked on. Everything inside me wanted to run away, to retreat to somewhere dark and quiet. I felt like a piece of livestock up for auction, as if the crowd only saw what parts of me they would enjoy the most.

He led me over to the dartboard, where I did the same pose as during practice. Hips cocked to one side, hands on my hips and a massive smile.

"Melody's about to demonstrate to y'all how we like to warm up," Syko declared, twirling those knives so fast they just looked like flashes of silver light in the corner of my eye.

The whimsical music kicked up, and I remained as still as a statue, focusing on the Ferris wheel in the distance. In the fading daylight, it looked so beautiful and romantic. Inside, I froze with the realization that the magic and beauty of the carnival was all an illusion. The drunk man with the creepy leer across the stage. That was the reality.

Thunk! Thunk! Thunk! Thunk!

Dead silence filled the air for a mere second before the crowd erupted into cheers. Only then did I move, shifting my pose to demonstrate how closely Syko's blades landed without touching me.

The pinstripe-suited man approached me with a look of feigned worry on his face.

"I didn't ruin your outfit, did I, honey?"

"Good as new!" I chirped, looking out across the audience. My cheeks ached from smiling so much.

"Excellent!" Syko took my hand and raised it above our heads. "Give it up for Melody, everybody!"

An even louder cheer erupted and for a split second, I didn't want to hide. A rush of adrenaline filled me. Having sharp objects thrown at me in front of dozens of people gave me a rush, a high unlike anything else. They loved me. They were mesmerized. Maybe this illusion wasn't so bad after all. They came here to be entertained, and that was exactly what they were getting.

"Why don't we," Syko turned to me, suggestively pinning my hand against the board, "turn things up a notch, darlin'?"

"Ooh!" I shimmied my shoulders and winked at the audience, embracing the character I came up here to play. "I like the sound of that!"

He made a satisfied grunting sound, which I ignored. The audience's cheers became lewd, sending out wolf whistles and suggestive hand gestures, which I also chose to ignore. It was all in good fun. I just had to play along.

Syko produced the colorful silk scarves from his pockets with a flourish. "It ain't that kind of magic show, folks!" he bellowed, receiving raucous laughter in return.

He turned to me and I stepped on the wooden pegs sticking out from the dartboard, holding onto the edges for stability. When he came within inches of my face, scarves in hand, a coldness washed over me like being dunked in ice.

The energy in the surrounding air shifted, and I froze. This no longer felt like a harmless, playful game.

Syko pinned both of my wrists against the board and he squeezed hard. Too hard.

Oh shit, oh shit. Oh no.

I tried to wiggle but he wouldn't loosen his hold. Instead, he stepped in closer so his body pinned me to the board. His erection pressing against my lower stomach sent my mind panicking.

Then he smothered my mouth with his own.

❦ 6 ❦

MELODY

He was seriously kissing me in front of everyone! What the fuck? Why?

My mind reeled as I closed my mouth and tried to wriggle away. But he just pried my lips open again with his long, slimy tongue. He had me trapped with nowhere to run.

"Stop squirmin' and at least pretend to like it," he growled in my ear. "Or I'll give you something to bitch about later." To the audience, it probably looked like he was whispering some sweet nothings to me.

I froze like a statue again, still trying to reconcile what the actual fuck was happening.

"Smile. Laugh," he whispered threateningly. "Give them a show, you dumb slut."

Blinking back tears, I forced my facial muscles to pull my lips back into a grin that felt like a painful grimace. All I wanted was for this to be over.

The crowd continued with their suggestive cheers and wolf whistles, obviously immune to my discomfort. I searched their eyes, lingering on the women in the crowd. The wives, girlfriends, and groups of friends together. Surely they could see what just happened? They could at least tell me I wasn't going crazy and imagining things. But none of them looked back at me. Not one person really saw *me*, but just a prop on stage.

Syko took his time tying the scarves around my wrists and ankles, helping himself to groping me at every opportunity and not even bothering to hide it. While the insides of me crumpled and dried up like pieces of paper eaten by fire, I forced the outside to giggle and smile. To go along with his act with no consequence.

No one watching even seemed to question it. Not the musicians, the assistants, nor the other performers waiting for their cue to go on after us. Everyone just watched and stood around with blank expressions while this gross older man violated me in front of a captive audience.

Every second felt like an hour as we got through the spinning dartboard part of the act. My stomach roiled, and I knew it wasn't from the spinning. I needed to get away from here. Part of me wished one of Syko's knives would land right between my eyes so this nightmare could just end.

He finally untied me without issue. The stage, the eyes, and the Ferris wheel spun around and around in a dizzying circle, but I still plastered a smile on my face and did a little curtsy to thunderous applause. The stage hands swiftly removed the dartboard, and we took our exit.

"Now..."

Syko took hold of my upper arm and started to pull me the moment we were out of sight, but I was already prepared. I yanked my arm away and took off running. I didn't know where or how far to go. I just had to get away.

But on my stupid, ridiculous heels, I didn't make it very far.

I tripped and fell, landing on soft muddy grass and couldn't hold it in any longer. My stomach heaved, and I emptied everything I ate that day onto the grass. Even after I threw everything up, I coughed and dry-heaved as if that would help purge the feeling of Syko's mouth and hands on me. If I could only throw away my body and grow a new one, I would.

Then the tears came. Ugly, wracking sobs of fear, frustration, and embarrassment. I was still on carnival grounds somewhere, looking stupid and pathetic. I was no stranger to gross men, so why couldn't I keep it together? Why'd I run away like a baby? Guys like that were part of everyday life. I had no choice but to learn to deal with them.

I wiped my mouth with a shaking hand and looked down at the muddy, vomity mess of my clothes. A wave of despair brought forth more tears. Why the fuck did I think I could come out here and be a successful bombshell carnival performer? I was homeless Alabama trailer trash. Getting paid to deal with men like Syko was probably the best I'd be able to do.

"Hey."

I jumped, so startled that I landed on my butt again. I'd been so deep in my pity party that I didn't notice anyone walk up to me.

A man walked quickly toward me, his bronzed skin illuminated by all the lights from the rides and game booths. When he got closer, I saw dark green eyes, a furrowed brow, and a serious, unsmiling face.

Stilts. The amazing stilt-walking acrobat who was an asshole to everyone. He looked angry, but I was too weak to even try crawling away from him.

"Have some water."

My eyes followed the length of his arm to the sealed water bottle he held out to me.

I accepted it with a weak, shaky hand. "Thanks."

He nodded and looked away. I suddenly felt drenched in shame. Probably the most attractive man I'd ever seen in real life, and not only because he told Syko where to shove it, was looking at me sitting in the mud next to my vomit. I wanted to sink into the ground and never see the light of day again.

"You can shower and clean up in that trailer there." He pointed to a cluster of RVs. I recognized the one I first met with Mr. Fisher and Madame Tetons earlier in the day. So I was close to the main entrance.

"Thanks... again," I said weakly. The confusion piled onto my burning embarrassment and shame. Why was this guy helping me? Did he see me run off and come after me? Or did he just happen to find poor little me puking my guts out?

He cleared his throat awkwardly, as if he'd rather be anywhere else. "Are you hurt? Do you need help getting up?"

"Um, no. I think I'm okay."

He nodded again and promptly walked off, leaving me there blinking. The whole interaction happened so quickly, I wondered for a moment if it really happened.

I twisted open the water bottle and took a few small sips. My throat felt raw as sandpaper, but the water was cool and refreshing. Feeling a tiny bit better, I pulled off my shoes and climbed shakily to my feet. Careful not to step in my vomit or any other mysterious substance on the grass, I walked barefoot to the trailer he pointed to.

A light was on inside, and I hesitated before turning the doorknob. Who did this trailer belong to?

It was clean and cozy inside, much like a typical RV when going camping. I never went camping, but I saw commercials about it on TV before. A few books and maps filled a bookshelf. Towels, linens, and a few changes of clothes filled another shelf. A pair of metal crutches were wedged between the driver's seat and the shelf. I grabbed a towel and quickly hurried to the small standing shower in the back, feeling like I invaded someone's home.

I tried to shower as quickly as I could while still scrubbing my skin raw, washing off every sensation of Syko touching me. When I finally felt clean, I toweled off and wondered what the hell I was going to do about clothing. No way was I putting that muddy, vomit-covered outfit back on. Nor was I leaving this place wearing just a towel.

With the towel wrapped around me, I located trash bags to throw the soiled outfit in and hesitantly ran my hand along the T-shirts and shorts folded neatly on the shelf.

I'm just going to borrow them for tonight. If I bring them back, it won't be stealing, I thought.

I hastily made my decision, pulling out a soft gray shirt and pair of basketball shorts. Obviously made for a man, they hung like a pair of tents on my skinny frame.

I hoisted the trash bag filled with dirty clothes over my shoulder and made out like a thief in the night. Now that some time had passed and with my head cleared from the shower, I felt a little calmer as I walked to the dressing tent. With the show still going on, no one was around, which I was grateful for.

I dumped the bag in a trash can I walked past, figuring no one would want to bother cleaning the outfit. Quickly entering the tent and locating my backpack, I grabbed it and left again within seconds. With my own worn-out but comfortable shoes on my feet, I left the carnival grounds without looking back.

The homeless shelter was dark and quiet as I crept back to my assigned room I shared with a few other girls. Collapsing on my bunk bed, I only stared at the top bunk for a few seconds before drifting off, utterly exhausted from the day's events.

A few hours later I jolted awake, still on top of my sheets and wearing a stranger's shirt and shorts. With a groan, I flipped over to rummage through my pack for my pajamas. After a minute of fumbling with my zipper, I groaned and gave up. All I wanted to do was sleep for days. I'd be washing and returning these clothes, anyway.

I pulled back the covers and settled myself underneath them. Right before falling asleep again, I lifted the gray cotton T-shirt to my nose and took a small whiff. It smelled...nice. I couldn't place the woodsy, slightly earthy scent, but it was relaxing and comforting. And the shirt felt so nice and soft. For a brief moment, I felt what could only resemble safety and comfort.

I drifted off and slept hard for hours.

❈ 7 ❈

MELODY

My heart crashed painfully against my sternum as I stood frozen in front of the trailer door. For some reason, my hand refused to raise up and knock.

I woke up early that morning, reluctantly peeling off the borrowed clothes that embraced me as I slept during the night. After washing them in the sink, they only took an hour to air-dry in the heat. And now, folded in my arms just as neatly as I found them, I was afraid of meeting their true owner.

I was being stupid, I knew that. But what happened with Syko had me afraid of my own shadow. Just walking across the street back to this place had me on edge. This could be nothing or it could be Syko's own trailer, and who knew if he wanted to finish what he started? If he dragged me inside, no one would be able to help me then. The thought sent my nerves into panic mode again.

Still, I couldn't just stand here forever. Nor could I keep the clothes, however soft and comfortable they were.

I raised my fist and knocked.

"GO AWAY!" bellowed the voice from inside.

I jumped at the sudden shout, but quickly recovered.

"Um, I'm just returning your clothes," I called nervously through the door. "I needed to wear something clean after I took a shower. I hope that's okay."

Some rustling and unintelligible words came through. I remained frozen, listening eagerly but still no one came to the door. I was just about to place the clothes on the doorstep and leave when the door burst open.

Deep, forest-green eyes narrowed at me.

"You're back," a familiar, throaty voice said, sounding unamused.

Stilts. Of course, this was his trailer. My face flamed at the embarrassing *duh* moment. Why else would he say I could shower here? Still, the revelation surprised me. With that intense stare and permanent scowl, he didn't seem like the type to keep such a tidy, cozy space.

And his shirt. I slept in it. That meant it smelled like *him*.

"Yeah, just to return these." I thrust my arms full of clothing out toward his chest, which I just then realized was bare and *holy shit*.

His biceps were easily as big as my thighs, maybe even bigger. Those arms and shoulders looked like they could crush a man's head, not to mention that chest and abs which looked carved from bronze itself. Of course, he had to be strong and athletic to do his performing, but I didn't expect him to be built like that. A faded tattoo was inked on the left side of his chest, the symbol familiar to me, but I couldn't quite place it. An eagle sitting on top of a globe with an anchor behind it.

He looked at the pile of clothes in my hands and cocked an eyebrow, like they were the last thing he wanted to touch.

"I washed them," I said. He didn't need to know that I slept in them. "Thanks again for letting me use your shower."

"Thanks for not being a thief," he mumbled.

Before I could react, he yanked the clothes from my hands, withdrew back inside, and slammed the door shut.

"You're fuckin' welcome," I mumbled, shaking my head as I descended the rickety stairs.

"Ah, miss Melody!"

I looked to see Mr. Fisher hurrying down the steps of his own trailer.

"Hi, Mr. Fisher," I greeted with a tight smile. Did he know what happened last night?

"Madame Tetons and I couldn't find you after the show last night," he said. "I wanted to make sure you got paid for your work." He produced a plain white envelope that was nearly an inch thick, and my eyes widened. Even if that was stuffed with singles, I didn't expect to make nearly that much.

"Thanks," I said, taking the envelope and tucking it under my arm.

"We had a record turnout last night!" he exclaimed excitedly. "It might've been the Wolf Man hype, but I heard your show got a little wild and steamy." He winked and bile rose in my throat.

"Uh, yeah." I forced out a laugh. "It was... *fun*."

"Well, I'm sorry to say you won't be working with Syko tonight," he said. "The burlesque show is the focus tonight. We need a rowdy, tipsy crowd. You'll be helping the bartenders in the booze tent." He must have noticed my hesitation and gave me a long look. "You *were* planning on working again tonight, right?"

I opened my mouth to say no.

I didn't want to come within a hundred feet of Syko again. And if everyone else had no issues with encouraging his disgusting display, then he definitely wasn't the only one who would do it. I ran away from home to free myself from monsters, not to run right back into their den.

But my fingertips squeezed the envelope of cash, gauging the thickness of it. No matter what, I would need more. This envelope would get thinner and thinner until it ran out. I needed more, lots more money if I was going to get by.

I didn't even have a goal or a plan, I just wanted to make it to the next day. I'd have to keep working and keep dealing with men like Syko because they were everywhere. If I could hide behind a bar, that would probably be the best work day I could hope for.

So I smiled and said, "Of course! When do you need me here?"

He told me and directed me to where the booze tent would be set up. I thanked him and began walking off the carnival grounds again, but not before I saw a curtain move in Stilts' trailer window in the corner of my eye.

I went to the thrift store down the street and spent most of my money on new clothes. The last of my money I splurged on a huge breakfast at McDonald's and a prepaid cell phone. Not that I had anyone to call, but it might come in handy if I wanted to get any other jobs.

It wasn't until I was back at the shelter, relaxing on my

bed and playing a game on my new phone, that I thought of my lucky coin.

"Fuck!" I sat up like a lightning bolt hit me and began tearing through all my belongings. "No, no, no..."

I dumped everything I owned out on my bed and rummaged through it five times over. Then I looked underneath the bed and began crawling on the floor. I patted myself down, even looking in my bra and underwear. Nothing.

"Goddamn it!" I threw myself on the bed in frustration and willed myself not to cry.

I couldn't explain why I was so attached to that thing, aside from that it was the only thing ever freely given to me with no strings attached. When I was little, it was magical to me. The magician pulled it out from behind my ear!

As I got older, I knew that was a trick, but it was no less special to me. It was mine and no one else's. I didn't have to share it with my siblings and no one tried to take it from me, which made me treasure it.

Rubbing my forehead, I thought back to when I last had it. I shoved it down my corset before going onstage. With a groan, I rubbed my eyes. I'd forgotten all about it during Syko's show. For all I knew, he could have reached in there and stolen it. Everywhere he touched me, I was just trying to ignore that it was happening.

And if not there, it could have fallen out while I was running. Or when I fell.

I had to face it. The only thing I owned with any sentimental value was gone.

I sighed and flipped violently over onto my stomach. It

didn't seem to matter if I was back home or out in the real world. Life was shitty at every turn.

MELODY

"How old are ya, sweet thing?"

"Eighteen," I replied tersely.

I was getting a little tired of everyone asking for my age but thankfully Higgins, the booze tent boss or BTB as he was called, didn't look at me with the same creepy leer as Syko. Instead, he seemed disgruntled, which was perfectly fine with me.

"I ain't lookin' to get my goddamn liquor license taken away again," he snarled. "So you ain't servin' nobody til you're twenty-one, girlie. You can clean glasses and restock. Don't worry, you'll still get cash tips."

"Sounds great! Where do I start?"

His gray caterpillar eyebrows raised in amusement but I was being completely serious. I was great at cleaning up alcohol, I'd been doing it since I could reach Mom's kitchen sink on my little footstool. And not serving meant I didn't have to interact with the patrons as much. No, I was perfectly happy to keep my head down, make everything spotless, and not talk to anyone.

Higgins seemed to warm up to me as I followed him behind the bar, listening intently as he showed me where everything was stored and the proper cleaning procedures. Because we didn't have a sink with running water in the tent, three buckets were set up to wash, rinse, and sanitize the various drinking glasses. A few small refrigerators powered by a generator kept the beers and chilled pint glasses. Ice was kept in a cooler, and liquor bottles lined a fully stocked cabinet behind the bar.

"And stay out of the bartenders' way," Higgins growled. "I don't need broken glass all over the damn place 'cause they keep running into the new girl."

"Not a problem," I grinned. "Does anything need washing or restocking right now?"

He directed me to two bussing tubs filled with used beer glasses. Apparently the bar back didn't show up last night, so they fell behind on cleaning. I scrubbed the glasses in the buckets, zoning out while Higgins manned the bar for the early patrons—mostly dads sneaking away for a quick beer or shot while the wives and kids rode the Ferris wheel and played at the game booths.

"Down a person again, Higgs?" asked one guy, nursing a beer while he eyed me.

"Two," Higgins grumbled. "My damn bartender is AWOL again. Kids these days, I swear to fuckin' God. At least tonight's bar back is actually doin' her damn job, but I'm not gettin' my hopes up."

It didn't take long for me to find out who the missing bartender was. A girl breezed in, who I recognized as one of Cherry's friends from the dressing tent. She wore a similar outfit as last night with a corset, short skirt, stockings, ridiculous heels, and a tiny top hat fixed to her hair.

With her face full of makeup and her tits pushed up to create ample cleavage, she was sure to be rolling in tips tonight.

Her cheery smile disappeared the instant she saw me, turning down into a scowl. I bristled with annoyance. What was she so pissed about?

Higgins didn't seem to notice or care about her obvious disdain toward me.

"Yer late, Leeann," he growled at her. "Quit starin' at the bar back and get yer ass to work. I'm behind on tomorrow's order now."

"Sorry, BTB," she said flippantly. "I had to cheer up a friend 'cause some skanky bitch tried to steal her man." She stared daggers at me when she said it, and I nearly dropped the armful of glasses I carried.

Seriously? *That's* what Cherry told her? What about the fact that her man was a sleazy asshole who touched me everywhere without permission and basically threatened me to go along with it?

I saw red as I stuck the glasses in the fridge, clinking them together with more force than was necessary.

"Hey, what did I say about breakin' them glasses?" Higgins bellowed at me.

"Sorry, BTB," I mumbled, forcing myself to be gentler. I could feel Leeann's sneer like an itch on my back.

As it turned out, I excelled at staying out of the way. I made sure to put as much distance between Leeann and myself as possible while still performing all of my duties. Unfortunately, she took every opportunity to make my job hell.

"None of these glasses are cleaned properly," she complained, dumping an armful into a bussing tub. "I'm not going to sacrifice my tips because the bar-bitch can't do her job!"

Whatever. I rewashed them without complaint.

"This bar is sticky!" she whined, wrinkling her nose as she tapped her fingers down on the bar top. "Customers need a clean place to sit. What the hell are you doing?"

I said nothing and wiped down the already spotless bar again.

"Why are there still empty glasses out on the pub tables?" she demanded. "You need to bus the tables and wipe them down!"

"Because I've been busy washing the other glasses a second time," I said with all the calmness I could muster.

As dusk faded to night outside, the tent became busier, buzzing with late patrons here to enjoy the second day of the freak show. Thankfully, Leeann was kept busy tending the bar and left me in peace. It got so busy that Higgins came from the back to help out.

Without Leeann biting my ankles, I got into a good rhythm of washing, drying, and wiping up messes. Snippets of conversation floated my way as I walked through the tent to pick up empty glasses.

"He gave another whole five minutes about the damn Wolf Man again. What do you think that is?"

"It's a fuckin' hoax. Probably ain't nothin' at all. They just want us to keep comin' back and spendin' money."

"Hey, kid!" Higgins snarled when I returned. I didn't think he bothered learning my name. "You know how to pour a beer from the tap?"

"Uh, yeah," I said, confused. "But I thought you didn't want me to-"

"Fuck the liquor laws! I got a fuckin' line goin' out the

door and too many fuckin' mojitos to make! Start a beer line and take care of those people!"

"What?! But she's going to get a cut of my tips!" Leeann whined over the growing noise of the crowded tent.

"She was gonna get a cut anyway, now shut the fuck up and do yer job!"

"Hey!" I cupped my hands around my mouth to yell over the crowd. "If you're in line for a beer, come and see me!"

The line branched off and veered toward me. We broke out the plastic cups for people to take outside the tent, which made things a lot faster. I worked so fast, I just threw whatever tips they left into another empty glass. By the time the line disappeared, my feet ached and my tip jar overflowed with dollar bills.

"Nice work, kid," Higgins said, snapping a dishrag over his shoulder. "You really know how to hustle and you showed up on time." He shot a glare over at Leeann. "If you want a job here tomorrow, you're welcome to it."

"Thanks!" I said earnestly, gulping down a glass of water. "I'll be here tomorrow, then."

He nodded with a grunt. "We got a couple hours left, so take it easy. The performers will be coming in as their shows finish. Help yourself to a drink but don't get sloppy."

"Thanks," I said again. *But no thanks*, I thought.

Working at a bar was fine with me, but the stuff would never touch my lips. Just seeing how my mom and older sister turned out gave me enough reason to abstain from booze entirely.

I drained the rest of my water and began cleaning up

my area. When someone took the seat in front of me, I looked up with a plastered smile to find myself staring into a pair of forest green eyes and an extremely kissable pair of lips surrounded by dark stubble.

"Whiskey with ice," those lips said gruffly. "Please," he added.

I froze in my tracks for two reasons. First because my muscle memory was confused that this wasn't a beer order. Second, because the man sitting in front of me was none other than Stilts. It seemed like forever ago that he slammed his trailer door in my face. Was that really just this morning?

"Coming right up!" I chirped, unfreezing from my stupor and pulling out a whiskey tumbler.

I had no idea how much ice I was supposed to add, so I filled it about three-fourths full and topped it off with roughly two fingers of Jack Daniels. He took it from me without comment, to my relief.

"How much?" he grumbled.

"Oh, don't worry about it." I waved my hand away at the wad of cash he produced. "This one's on me."

He lifted an eyebrow while his lips pressed into a thin, tight line.

"And why're you buyin' my drink, miss?"

"For the other night," I lowered my voice. "Just to say thanks for the water and letting me shower at your place." My eyes dropped bashfully. "That was really nice and unnecessary, so thank you."

"It was nothing," he protested, his voice a low, sexy growl. "Let me pay for the drink."

"No, I told you," I argued. "It's my way of saying thanks."

"Look, I'm leaving this here." He slapped a twenty down on the bar. "Charge me for the drink or take the whole thing as a tip. I don't care. I didn't help you, so you could owe me anything in return. I'm paying for the drink, your service, or both."

I cocked my head, trying not to stare too much despite him being very nice to look at.

"I don't know what you're getting so bent out of shape for. It's *one* drink. I'm just trying to say thank you."

"You're welcome." He stubbornly pushed the bill toward me, and I made no move to touch it. With another frustrated yet sexy growl, he picked up his whiskey and took a long swig.

"My name's Melody," I offered, wiping down the counter next to him. "What's yours?"

"Stilts." He glared at me defiantly, but I swore I could see a hint of playfulness there. Just my luck that the kindest person to me in this carnival was this stubborn, curmudgeonly, but gorgeous man.

"Alright, be that way," I shot back, holding back the girlish giggle threatening to bubble up from my chest.

He rolled his eyes and returned to his whiskey, but his lips twitched as if he was hiding back a smile, too.

Rotten luck in life was nothing but second nature to me at this point. Considering today was a pocket full of sunshine compared to last night, I felt confident enough to laugh at my shitty luck tonight. Maybe even push its buttons a little.

"You in the military?" I asked, noticing the silver dog tags around his neck.

"You always ask so many damn questions?" he fired back.

"It's called having a conversation," I teased. Something told me this guy was all bark and no bite. "It's what people do when they go to bars."

"Well, excuse me, Miss Melody," he hissed through gritted teeth. "I've had a long-ass day turning tricks like a show pony for an asshole boss and hundreds of degenerates who conveniently forget that I'm a person on that stage. So if you don't mind, I'd like to enjoy the drink I *bought* in peace."

Well, shit. Clearly, I misread him.

"Sorry," I mumbled, quickly gathering up glasses to wash. "The drink is still free, though."

My confidence deflated and my cheeks burning, I hurried away from the bar to give the guy his much-needed space. But I couldn't escape Leeann's sneer as I bent over the washing buckets.

"Nice try, there. Keep at it," she scoffed. "He's an asshole so you two deserve each other."

Jaw clenched, I ignored her and continued on with my washing.

"I heard he's gay, too," she went on. "Every girl in the carnival has tried to ride his dick, but he always tells 'em to fuck off. Plus, he's just too pretty to be straight."

"Maybe he actually has standards," I muttered under my breath. Not that I thought in a million years I had a chance with him, or even wanted one. I just wanted to learn a little about the person who extended some kindness to me.

I thought he might at least want to be friends. But again, I was wrong.

"The fuck is that supposed to mean?" Leeann screeched.

"Nothing. Shit."

She didn't escalate further, and I silently begged her to go away. A group of young guys came in, shattering the peaceful silence, and she flounced over to them, tossing her hair and making her voice high and flirtatious. I took a deep breath and forced myself to tune everything out.

After washing yet another batch of glasses, I wiped my hands dry and looked up just in time to see Stilts finish his whiskey. His forest green eyes caught mine and did not let go.

Steeling myself, I marched back over to my place in front of him.

"Another one?"

"No." He set the glass down. "Thank you, Melody." His tone was gentler than mere moments ago.

"You can call me Mel." The words tumbled out automatically, and I bit my tongue too late.

"Alright, Mel." He slid out of his barstool and paused. "It's Connor."

I looked up. "What?"

"My name," he said, "is Connor."

He turned and I watched his broad, muscle-bound back stride out of the tent.

9

MELODY

The booze tent was even more crowded the next night. On top of pouring beers, Higgins had me mixing basic cocktails. By my twentieth Jack and Coke, my tip jar was stuffed to the brim and overflowing. My feet killed me and there seemed to be constant drips of sweat running down my temples. But as long as I was out of reach of every man who leered at my tits shoved into my leather corset, I was happy to continue.

Leeann however, didn't let up in making my job miserable and because we were so busy, Higgins let one of her catty friends work behind the bar with us. One whispered remark between them and both girls looked at me like I crawled out of a sewer.

Whatever. I already accepted I wouldn't be making any friends in this place. Especially not with the girls. But I couldn't help but feel like learning Stilts' real name was a small victory.

I thought about him as I walked past his trailer on my way back to the shelter last night. His lights were on inside and I had an itch to knock at his door, just to bug him and find out what more I could learn.

But he'd likely demand what I wanted, and I didn't have an answer to give him. Even *I* had too much pride to confess he was the closest thing to a friend I had. What could I say? *Hey, I know your real name and I slept in your clothes once, so we're obviously like best pals now.*

So I fell asleep in my bottom bunk at the shelter with a small giggle in my throat as I tried out his name on my lips.

"Connor." I whispered it to my pillow like a secret, wondering if anyone else knew.

I remembered this secret, repeating it in my head like a mantra, when Leeann and her friend accidentally-on purpose began throwing drinks at me. They aimed at my legs and only did it when directly behind the bar so no one would see. To anyone sitting at the bar, it looked like they were dumping out melted ice and used-up garnishes into bussing tubs.

My legs and shoes were sticky and disgusting within minutes, but I still ignored them. I thought of the person who gave water to a girl kneeling in the mud, covered in her own vomit. If people like him existed, I wouldn't sink to the level of these two catty bitches.

A lull in customers gave me an opportunity to rinse my legs off with a hose. I sprayed myself quickly and patted my legs dry with a towel, swiveling my head around to keep an eye out for Bitch One and Bitch Two. They were at the far end of the bar, talking to someone leaning on his forearms. Leeann laughed at something he said, tossing her bleached hair over her shoulder, and my blood froze when I saw who she was talking to.

Syko. But just seeing him wasn't the only source of my shock. Someone had fucked him up.

His left eye was swollen shut and surrounded by an eggplant-purple bruise. He held a bag of crushed ice to his jaw and his lower lip was split in half. I forgot I was staring until his beady black eyes bore into mine over Leeann's shoulder and he scowled.

I sprung into action, my heart nearly exploding in my chest as I moved quickly, darting my eyes away and returning to my work with shaking hands. Time seemed to slow to a crawl as I tried to quell my panic with deep breaths.

Calm down, calm down. There's people here. He wouldn't...

I shook my head and huffed out a laugh at myself. We were in front of hundreds of people the last time he put his filthy hands all over me. Clearly, being seen wasn't a fear of his.

But the seconds crawled on as I tried my best to ignore him, and he seemed to be doing the same. The girls resumed serving customers, and he stayed put at the far end of the bar, drinking heartily from his flask. I breathed a little more freely as it became clear he had no intention of moving from his spot. All the easier to stay the hell away.

I got so preoccupied in scrubbing my glasses, I didn't notice someone took the seat in front of me until a rich, velvety voice spoke.

"No twenty here on the bar. I guess you took it after all?"

Stilts! No, *Connor*. He came back. His face was still unsmiling, but his eyes were playful.

"I donated it to the homeless shelter across the street,"

I said. That was the truth. I dropped it in the donation box up front before going to bed last night.

A hint of a smile cracked the rugged, hard expression on his face. "Seriously? You're just as stubborn as me, girl. You should learn to take something when it's dropped in your lap."

"So should you," I retorted. "Especially when that something is a thank you."

He groaned and hid his mouth behind his hand, but I could tell he was trying to hide a laugh.

"Anyway, what can I get you?" I offered. My heart lifted that he came back again. Maybe he wasn't as pissed off the other night as I thought.

"I'll just have a beer this time. It's hot as fuck and I'm dyin' for something refreshing." He took his hands off the bar and set them in his lap, leaning forward like he was adjusting his boots.

"There's always water for that," I teased, but grabbed a chilled glass and began pouring.

"Beer is ninety percent water, *Melody*," he shot back. His eyes narrowed, but a smile still tugged at his lips. "Do you always give customers such a hard time?"

"Just you, *Connor*," I retorted before I could think. My face heated as I turned away for a moment. Holy shit, was I flirting?

His handsome face finally broke out into a full-on grin, and my heart skipped a beat. A light blush even tinged his cheekbones pink. Sweet baby Jesus, he was even more gorgeous when smiling.

I placed the beer in front of him and tried not to read into his fingers, brushing mine. *No, Mel,* I scolded myself.

You're not going to turn into a giggling idiot just because of a guy. Not even if he's a really hot guy.

"It's four dollars. You can actually pay for this one," I continued to tease.

"My, my. Never thought I'd see the day." He dropped a five on the bar. "Keep it, babe."

"Thanks."

My skin tingled delightfully upon hearing the pet name like it was a caress. The exact opposite reaction I felt from everything Syko called me. He could have called me every sweet name in the book and it would still make my skin crawl. These two men sitting at opposite ends of the bar seemed to perfectly illustrate the wide spectrum of humanity.

Speaking of which, Syko just then seemed to notice Connor sitting in front of me. His scowl grew even more twisted, and he hunched further over his flask, barking something at Leeann, which sounded like another drink order.

"He been bothering you any more?" Connor's gaze burned intensely into mine, the sexy smile gone.

"No. He's been staying far away, thankfully." All my flirtatious confidence zapped away in that moment. I lowered my eyes shamefully and absently wiped a glass with a cloth over and over. "So you saw that too, huh?"

"The tail end of it, yeah. I saw you run away like the hounds of hell were after you."

A thought made my hands freeze. I looked to my right again. Syko threw back a shot of something and applied a fresh bag of ice to his swollen jaw. I then looked back at Connor, his face expressionless as he sipped his beer pensively. The knuckles on his hand had faint bruises and appeared slightly swollen.

"Did you..." I lowered my voice to a whisper, angling my head in Syko's direction. "Did you have something to do with his face looking like that?"

"I ain't his dad so, no. I'm not responsible for that ugly motherfucker."

"You know what I mean." I narrowed my eyes.

Connor set his beer down and swallowed. His Adam's apple bobbed and my lips parted with the mental image of kissing it.

"Again, the answer is no." His expression didn't change, but his eyes danced with mischief.

"Why's your hand swollen?" I pressed.

"It's from my act. Doing handstands and swinging on bars and shit."

He wasn't going to give me a different answer, no matter what I asked. I almost wished I felt conflicted and weird about it, but I didn't.

Syko deserved it. If I was big and strong enough, I would have fucked his face up myself. I had no sympathy for him and would never condemn Connor for doing that, as much as I hated violence. The only part that confused me was *why*. But for some reason, I didn't feel ready to ask that question.

"So how'd it go today?" I said, eager for a lighthearted subject change.

"Same old shit," he mumbled into his beer. The question seemed to make him sullen, like he'd rather talk about anything else. He reached under the bar again and grimaced as he seemed to massage a cramp in his leg.

"All the stilt tricks tough on your legs?" I asked sympathetically.

"You could say that." He answered with a low growl. It didn't sound like he wanted to talk about anything regarding work. "How'd you end up in this shithole, Mel?"

My insides did a somersault upon realizing he actually asked a question about me. "A nice state trooper drove me in, technically speaking."

His eyes narrowed in confusion. "Why would he do that?"

"I ran away from home and was living at a rest stop for a week," I answered casually.

His eyebrows shot up. "Really? You're a tougher chick than you look, then." He sounded impressed and my imaginary feathers ruffled proudly. Speaking softer, he added, "Home was a rough place for you then, huh?"

"You could say that." I mimicked his dismissive answer, feeling just as eager to talk about my home life as he was about his work life.

"Fair enough," he relented.

A brief silence passed between us as both of our gazes shifted to the opposite end of the bar. Syko was nowhere to be seen, and my shoulders sagged with relief.

"Don't let your guard down yet, babe," Connor muttered under his breath. "That shifty fucker might be up to something. I wouldn't put it past him."

"You're right," I muttered back, feeling my spine go rigid again. Even though all the creepy signs were there, Syko deliberately waited to really humiliate me until I was onstage and literally tied up so I couldn't escape. Lots of men were creepy without being straight-up predators. I wouldn't make the mistake of thinking he was harmless again.

"Hey you, girl!" Leeann screeched from the back of the tent. "Get over here!"

I rolled my eyes. Of course, she wouldn't bother to learn my name.

"Coming!" I hollered back, drying my hands. "Be right back," I said to Connor.

"Won't be soon enough." He said it so softly as I walked away, I thought I must've misheard him as I pushed back the rear tent flap.

"The fuck are you smirking for?" Leeann's bitchy friend demanded.

"Nothing," I sighed. "What do you need?"

The two wore their best cunty glares with their arms folded under their breasts, staring down their noses at me through heavy false lashes.

"Stay away from Syko, you dumb whore," Leeann spat. "After all she did to help, you repay Cherry by seducing her man?"

Stunned, my jaw dropped open.

"Are you fucking kidding me?" I demanded. "This bull-shit is what you dragged me out here for?"

"Why the fuck would we be joking?" Cunt Number Two shot back. "Cherry *loves* him. It's like, *real* love. She was about to tell him to stop pulling out so they could start a family. But you had to show up and shove your tits in his face!"

"Jesus tap-dancing Christ," I groaned, dropping my forehead to my palm. No matter where I went, trash seemed to follow me. "I can't believe I actually have to say this, but I don't want Syko. He's creepy, he's twice my age, and I sure as fuck did not wanting him touching me onstage!"

"Then why didn't you say no?" Leeann demanded, leaning forward into my face. "You sluts always whine about it afterward, but if you didn't like it, why the fuck didn't you stop it?"

"Are you serious?" I was incredulous, but still didn't want these bitches to know how much he scared me. "You're telling me you've *never* been in that position, Leeann?"

A glass shattering and voices yelling inside the tent made me spin around. Through the tent flap, I saw four men restraining Connor and barely at that. Two guys held back his massive arms and shoulders as he struggled. With just a bit more wiggling, he'd have one arm free.

I could only be taken aback by his strength for a split second before my panic kicked in.

"Connor!" I shrieked, running into the tent.

His green eyes, wide and dilated, caught mine as he paused for half a moment in his struggle. I saw the anger, the adrenaline pumping through them from the sudden attack, but also something else. Was that *fear* I saw?

"Get out of here, Melody!" he roared. "It's not safe! Go!"

"I'll get help!" I yelled, rounding the bar. "I'll find Higgins!"

"No! Just go!"

Running to his side of the bar, now filled with people looking to watch the fight, I noticed the figure kneeling at Connor's feet.

Syko rose to standing slowly, an evil grin spreading on

his face and a wooden baseball bat resting across his shoulders. My stomach collapsed in a pit of dread.

"I'll teach y'all how to fuck with me," he said softly, then swung the bat with all his might.

"NO!" I cried too late.

He aimed low across Connor's shins. The wooden bat made a loud *clank* as it connected with metal.

Wait, *what?*

In slow motion, Connor's lower legs and shoes seemed to rip away from under his pant leg. They rolled across the floor from the force and hit the bar with a thud and another clang.

Syko and his goons laughed uproariously while I stared in horror. The four guys holding Connor up dropped him without warning. He braced himself with his forearms but still landed hard and grunted from the impact. He quickly pulled himself across the ground to his prosthetic legs and I could only stare in shock and disbelief.

This man walked in stilts when his real legs ended at his knees.

10

CONNOR

I don't know what prompted me to go back to the booze tent that night. Or why I told her my real name the first night. That girl Melody was too wide-eyed, young, and naïve. She thought the carnival world was all cotton candy and deep-fried cheesecake. She was completely unaware of the corruption that poisoned this kind of job, the poison that got me here in the first place.

That naivete was exactly the reason Syko targeted her. Dickbags like him always spotted girls like her from a mile away, circling slowly around her like vultures. The poor thing never saw it coming.

I hated people who preyed on the weak. I saw it constantly in Afghanistan, which opened my eyes to how it happened more subtly back home. So after I caught up to her and offered her water and my place to shower, I put old Syko in his place after doing that shit onstage.

Honestly, I didn't beat him that hard. Just popped him a couple of times as a warning.

"Fuckin' gimp!" he cursed at me, spitting blood. "You

wouldn't be shit without those fuckin' robot legs."

"Touch that girl again," I said, "and I'll show you what I can do with no legs."

I went home after that, not sure of what I would find. Not that I would've been displeased with a naked girl in my shower, but she definitely wouldn't want to be around a man after what happened. And even if she did, she'd change her mind the moment my pants came off.

My place had been empty, the shower still wet, and a towel hung over the shower door. A mixture of relief and disappointment filled me. No one except me had been in this place since I bought it. The thought of a woman being in here using my shower felt absolutely alien.

A flash of something metallic caught my eye on the floor and I bent over to pick it up. It was some kind of coin or token, inlaid with gold and a silver ring around it. I didn't recognize the design—definitely not one of our carnival tokens.

The girl must have dropped it. Which was unfortunate, because I figured she'd never come back after that ordeal.

When she showed up at my door the next morning, my borrowed clothes folded neatly in her hands, I forgot all about returning her coin.

She looked up at me with those rich brown eyes, no longer weighed down with fake eyelashes and ridiculous makeup. Her pert, pink lips curved into a smile that no man like me would ever deserve.

And I fucking slammed the door in her face. I only took a moment to hold the shirt and shorts I snatched from her, wondering how long they touched her skin, when voices prompted me to look outside.

She was talking to the carnival manager, Mr. Fisher. Another perverted fuck, but too cowardly to actually pull shit off like Syko. He handed her an envelope and asked her a question I couldn't make out. She nodded, smiling back at him as she replied. A smile still full of naïve brightness and hope. Was this girl seriously going to keep working here? I couldn't decide if she was tougher or stupider than I thought.

I pushed my curtain back into place before they could see me. If she was sticking around, I could only hope Syko took my threat seriously.

When those big doe eyes looked at me from across the bar for the first time, you guessed it. I forgot all about giving her back the damn coin again.

She annoyed me with all her questions and attempts to start a conversation, or at least that was what I kept trying to convince myself. I was not *just* a closed book. I was a book sealed shut with a chain wrapped around it and thrown into the ocean to sink into the abyss. Nobody knew my background, my real name, and definitely not the status of my disability. Syko only knew because he drunkenly tried to stab me in the calf one time.

Classy people, my coworkers.

So I left the bar that first night, never intending to come back. She had my name now, and that already felt like too much.

But I had hers, too. She gave it to me freely, just like she gave me that drink.

Melody. Like a song.

And just like a song, I couldn't get her out of my head ever since then. All the more reason to stay far away from the booze tent.

My prosthetics were killing me after the show. I was on my way home to relax and get the damn things off when I spotted Syko making a beeline for the booze tent. I hesitated for just a second before turning around and following him.

My training in the Marines taught me to follow through on every promise I made. I told him there would be consequences for messing with Melody again and I had to see that through. It had nothing to do with how her doe eyes made my heart jump or the fact she'd been running through my head all day. A man's honor was keeping his word, and that was the sole purpose of following him.

I didn't want it super obvious to the old creep I was onto him, so I let myself talk and flirt with Melody. And goddamn it, I liked it.

I smiled for the first time in what felt like years. I even laughed a little. The girl was just as sweet as she was tough. I let my fucking guard down and just enjoyed the moment with her. It would never last, so I figured, *what's the harm in talking to a pretty girl?* By the time this shitshow of a carnival was over, I'd never see her again.

And this time, I wouldn't forget to give back her mysterious coin.

My finger traced across the face of it in my pocket. I kept it on me in the wide, bulky pants I wore during the show, which conveniently covered up my prosthetics down to my shoes. The coin never flew out during my routines, which miraculously went without any hitches in the last two nights. Maybe it was a good luck charm despite the aches in my limbs afterwards.

When Mel came back from talking to her two bitchy coworkers, I planned to flip it in the air and place it in her hand. Those doe eyes would light up and her cute little mouth would open in a gasp. I was near giddy with anticipation, waiting for her to come back. So much so that I didn't notice four of Syko's goons come up behind me and yank me off my stool.

"Well, this makes things an awful lot clearer, gimp," the ugly bastard sneered. "Yer sweet on that pretty little thing, ain't ya?"

"And you're still a big pussy," I hissed, struggling against the restraints, but they all twisted my arms behind my back. "You need four dudes to come at me? Too chickenshit to even face a gimp man-to-man?"

His smile dropped. Of fucking course he was, and he hated how I just said that in front of his boys.

He revealed the Louisville slugger from behind his back and pointed it straight at me.

"I'll teach ya to run yer fuckin' mouth on me, Stilts," he growled.

I stared him down, daring him to make good on his threat. If he cracked that thing over my head—well, the world wouldn't miss me. But a man like Syko could never bear the responsibility of taking another man's life. He was too much of a weasel for that. Like I thought he would, he kneeled to the ground, laid the bat next to him, and started fucking with my prosthetics.

"Let's hear you talk shit without yer fuckin' robot legs," he muttered, pulling and twisting on the silicone sleeves that held my legs in place.

"Go ahead and keep feeling me up, Syk," I said dryly. "You only get action when your victim's restrained so enjoy it while you can."

"Shut the fuck up. At least I still have a dick to play

with."

"Those tend to be pretty useless without any balls."

I still had a dick, too. I didn't know where he got the implication that I lost mine along with my legs, or if he was just really that stupid. Either way, I didn't give a shit about correcting him.

"Connor!"

Oh shit.

Melody ran back into the tent, her doe eyes wide and fearful. Fuck it all. Of all the people crowding around in this tent, she was the only one I cared about not seeing me like this. We wouldn't see each other after this carnival and I didn't want to alter her perception of me. I didn't want her to think of me as lesser.

"Get out of here, Melody!" I hollered. "It's not safe, go!"

Of course, she didn't listen. She rounded the bar to get closer and saw what Syko was doing, although she didn't understand yet.

I stopped struggling then. It was no use. Syko wouldn't hurt me, not badly. All I wanted was for her to not see me, and I was powerless to stop that from happening.

He swung my legs out from under me and his boys dropped me on my face. I still weighed a good two hundred pounds from the knees up and a shock rattled my forearms when I hit the ground. But at least I didn't hit my head.

Naturally, they laughed and pointed like a bunch of schoolyard bullies as I pulled myself across the floor to my legs. I didn't give a shit about them, but the last thing I wanted to do was look up and see the expression on Melody's face.

I pulled myself up to a sitting position and quickly began putting them on again. Higgins started shouting over the din, saying it was time to get the hell out. Syko gave me one last, disgusted look over his shoulder and spit on the ground in my direction before walking out of the tent, his boys following him obediently.

I scoffed and shook my head as I secured my prosthetics back into place. Even on the ground with nothing to modify me and he still wouldn't come at me. The best he could do was try to humiliate me. What a small, stupid man. If he ever bothered to stop and think for a minute, he might realize I'd seen and heard it all before.

"Connor."

A small hand rested gently on my forearm. Up close, Melody smelled like freshly blooming jasmine. But I couldn't bring myself to look at her.

"I told you to go, Melody," I barked as I snatched my arm away and grabbed a barstool to pull myself to standing.

"But he was going to-"

"Nothing," I snapped. "He didn't do shit 'cause he's a giant pussy. I had it handled. You should've gone."

I shouldn't have talked to her so harshly. She didn't do anything wrong. Nothing was hurt but my ego. Now she would see me as nothing more than a poor, pitiful creature. Just like everyone else did.

Who was I kidding? Vicky was right. No woman would ever want me after what happened.

"Almost forgot," I mumbled, reaching into my pocket. "Here. You dropped this."

I flipped the coin at her and began walking away before even seeing if she caught it or not.

11

MELODY

I gripped the coin in my fist, feeling like I had been standing outside Connor's door for hours. A bead of sweat trickled between my breasts, an indication I should get out of the blazing midmorning sun soon.

What am I doing here? It was not the first time the question popped into my head and I still didn't have an answer.

Last night was awful, and I just want to check on him.

Check for what? You saw that he didn't get injured. He's a grown man, he can handle some wounded pride.

The arguing with myself went around in circles. With a resigned sigh, I raised my fist and knocked at the flimsy door, making sure to squeeze my coin in my other hand for good luck.

"Go away!" came the muffled snarl through the door.

"Connor, it's me, Mel," I called.

"I fucking know that."

The words stung like acid flung at my skin. We had

been getting along so well last night until Syko had to prove himself the biggest asshole in the world. Now, it was like a switch had flipped and he was treating me like I was the one who wronged him.

"We don't have to talk about what happened," I tried again. "I just wanted to make sure we're good. That you're good." I bit my lip at my concern for him leaking through.

"Perfectly fine. Now go away."

"If that's true, why are you yelling at me through the door instead of talking to me face-to-face?"

"I don't want your pity, Melody."

"I don't pity you!" I cried out in frustration, maybe a bit too loudly. "I don't care about your... condition, or whatever. Honestly, I think it's amazing what you're able to do in spite of it."

He was silent for so long, with no movement inside the trailer. I pressed my ear to the door and said more quietly, "Connor?"

"Damn it. I thought you'd gone."

"Alright, fine!" I threw my hands up. "Hide in your trailer and be a coward, just like Syko, then!"

I stomped down his steps in a huff, my blood thumping in my ears. I was so mad I didn't hear his door swing open until he called out, "Melody!"

I turned around to see him standing in the doorway, wearing the same heather gray shirt I borrowed and loose-fitting sweatpants. The shirt hugged his biceps and chest like a second skin.

"Here, isn't this what you wanted?" he asked mockingly, spreading his arms out. "Come in and help yourself to a cup of tea, why don't you?"

Part of me had it up to here with his shit and wanted to keep walking the other way. But the other part didn't want to let this opportunity slip through my fingers. Who knew when he'd go back to hiding from the world? I wanted to learn more about this man, who could be so kind and selfless, then turn around and bite my head off in the same breath. He was like a beautiful wild animal who spooked when you got too close. At the moment, he was letting me in and I had to tread carefully.

He went back inside, leaving the door open, which I approached with careful, hesitant steps. I took a moment to look at the small living space from the doorway. It looked and felt so different from the one other night I'd been in here. Still clean and orderly, but it felt far more welcoming now in the morning light.

"Thanks for giving my coin back," I said awkwardly from the doorway, still with no idea what to say or why I was really here.

Connor glanced over his broad shoulder at me. "You comin' in or staying out? I don't want any damn cicadas in here."

Mumbling an apology, I stepped forward and pulled the door closed behind me. The space between us and in the RV in general got a whole lot smaller.

"You drink coffee?" Connor asked, pulling a pot out from under a coffee maker.

"Yes, thanks."

He waved the pot toward a small table with two chairs. "Have a seat."

I did so and accepted the steaming mug from him before he sat across from me. He moved so fluidly. Just watching him walk about the tiny space had me entranced. There was nothing robotic, jarring, or unnatural about the steps he took. If he was intent on keeping his secret hidden, he did a fine job of that until Syko exposed him.

"What's that coin mean to you, anyway?" he asked gruffly.

"It's kind of a good luck charm," I said, wrapping my hands around the mug. "I've had it ever since I was a kid. It's just the one thing I've had for so long." I lifted my mug to my lips. "Why, do you recognize it?"

"I can tell it's a carnival token. Don't know where from, though."

Silence stretched between us. With every passing moment, my anxiety grew over what he was thinking. Was he pissed at me for badgering him again? Was he just humoring me until I finally left?

"Why'd you help me out that first night?" I asked. The one burning question that plagued me since it happened.

"Because it was the right thing to do."

He didn't sound pissed. His voice was calm and even-tempered.

In that same tone, he asked me, "Why do you insist on barging into my life, Melody?"

"I'm sorry," I blurted out. "You're probably the only person who's gone out of their way to be nice to me. Not just at this carnival, but my whole life. I'm not trying to throw a pity party, it's just that after you did that... I wanted to learn more about you. I wanted to know why you were different from everyone else and I don't mean your legs—"

I stopped abruptly, realizing I was digging myself into a

hole. "But I can tell you don't like having me around, so I'll say hi to you in the booze tent and let that be it. I won't bother you anymore and I won't tell anyone about your... you know."

His sculpted arms crossed in front of his chest as I talked. When I was done rambling, he broke into a smile, the same one that made my heart skip a beat, and started laughing. At my confused expression, his laugh grew even louder.

"I don't dislike you, Melody," he began.

"Mel," I corrected.

"Mel," he repeated, smirking. "I gotta admit I've never met anyone like you, either. You never stop asking questions and trouble always seems to find you."

I dropped my eyes to look at my coffee. "Sorry."

"Don't be sorry, damn it."

I looked at him again, even more confused than before.

"My life has been," he paused to think of the word, "mundane. Mind-numbingly so, for the past two years. I perform, I keep to myself, I collect my cash, which dries up too fast for me to save it. Same shit, different day. But you." He shook his head as if in disbelief. "Somehow this skinny, doe-eyed girl has made my life interesting again."

"How?" I asked.

"By being *you*," he grinned. "Most people who get in my business back off as soon as I tell them to. But you keep poking the bear and won't run away when it roars at you. You're fearless in a way that's very refreshing." He cocked an eyebrow. "You're lucky I'm not Syko. Or any other of the fuckin' creeps around here."

I blinked at him. "I don't get it. You *like* me bugging you? You get so pissed off, though. And I'm definitely not fearless," I frowned. I was just desperate for work and apparently friendship, but I didn't voice that to him.

His smile dropped. "I'm not the easiest person to get along with, Mel. I've... been through some things, obviously." He gestured down to his legs. "I have a short temper. I get snappish and frustrated easily. But," he reached across the table and grabbed my hand with a surprisingly gentle touch, "I won't ever assault you like Syko did. I'll never come close to that."

"He didn't—"

"Don't you dare defend him," he cut me off with a snarl. "He absolutely did. I heard him threaten you. It doesn't matter if he didn't hurt you physically, he had no right to do that."

I swallowed and nodded.

"So," Connor sighed, "if you can handle my moodiness and don't treat me differently now that you know I'm only three-fourths of a man, I guess I'm okay with you tagging along with me."

"You're not three-fourths of a man," I blurted out.

"Watch it, kid," he said sternly. When I mumbled an apology, he playfully flicked my hand that he still held. "I'm kidding. Lighten up, Mel."

"So you don't mind me asking you questions?" I said hopefully.

"You can ask whatever you want." He said it lightheartedly, but his mouth tightened. "Doesn't mean I'm gonna answer."

I thought for a moment, sipping coffee while I filed through the many questions I had swirling in my mind, trying to pick the least invasive ones.

"How old are you?" I began.

"Twenty-five," he answered, lifting an eyebrow. "You?"

"Just turned eighteen a couple weeks ago."

"Damn," he muttered, visibly shuddering. "I figured you were young, but not *that* young. That makes what Syko did even worse."

"Where are you from, originally?" I asked, eager to get the subject off of my age.

"A little-ass town called Paris," he grinned. "Paris, Arkansas."

"I was about to say, you don't sound French," I snorted.

Connor chuckled, pleased with his joke. "How about you, Mel?"

"An even smaller town, most likely," I told him. "Waterford, Alabama."

Not that I was thrilled to talk about my hometown, but my chest still bloomed with the mere fact that he was asking me questions in return. A complete 180 from him yelling at me to go away just minutes earlier. That had to mean something.

"Let me guess." He quirked an eyebrow. "About as redneck as it gets?"

"Yeah," I admitted. "I graduated high school and haven't gotten pregnant yet. That's considered a success where I'm from."

"Yep, 'bout the same story here." Connor rubbed his jaw as his southern twang emerged. "I went to college in Florida. That was where I got some actual culture and education in me."

"I never even left the state before coming out here," I

confessed, feeling a pang of envy at all the fun and adventures he must've had while in college.

To kids like me, a higher education was basically a distant mythology. A far-off dream we could never hope to have. Teachers prattled on endlessly about how important it was to get a degree for a good job, but the best I could hope for was like I said—done with high school and not yet pregnant.

"What made you leave?" he asked, draining his coffee cup.

"Just a shitty home life," I said tersely.

He nodded as if in understanding of my situation. I had no idea if he really understood, but he didn't ask any more, which I appreciated.

"How'd you end up in this place?" I asked, taking a chance on a more personal question.

He huffed out a dry laugh. "It was either this or become one of the millions of disabled veterans living on the street. Wasn't a hard choice at the time."

"So you were in the military," I confirmed, my gaze resting on his dog tags again.

"Yeah, whole lotta good that did me," he scoffed and then winced. "Well, I shouldn't say it like that. My training did me good. Getting my legs blown off and the lack of support and benefits afterward wasn't great."

"I'm sorry," I mumbled.

Connor glared at me. "What did I say about pity? I don't need or want your sorrys, kid."

I bit my tongue before another apology could tumble out. "I know. I didn't mean it like that. It's just not fair."

"Life isn't fair." He leaned back, resting his elbows on

the back of his chair. "The sooner you realize that, the less disappointing life will be."

A flash of anger surged through me. "Oh, I know that well enough already. The first seventeen years of my life were completely unfair, but I got by and dealt with it until I could leave. Then I did. You're not *that* much older than me, Connor. You don't need to act all high and mighty and treat me like a kid. I get it. Probably more than you think."

My heart pounded, and I didn't even realize I clenched my fists until my palms hurt from my nails digging in. I was just tired of people treating me like I didn't know anything, like I couldn't handle myself.

Since I was twelve years old, I was essentially the only adult in the house. Cleaning, cooking, changing diapers, and paying what bills I could. Just because I was stuck in that endless loop and never saw the "real" world didn't mean I couldn't handle what it threw at me.

"Alright," Connor said quietly, rubbing his jaw with a smirk. "You are tougher and wiser than I gave you credit for. Didn't mean to assume, Mel."

I blinked, genuinely shocked at the admission. Most men didn't admit when they were wrong. If anything, they doubled-down and got even more pissed off because their precious ego was threatened. Connor was starting to surprise me in many ways.

"Having said that," I waved my hand a bit sheepishly. "I don't know about anything in this world. Carnival politics or whatever. Figuring it out on my own has been pretty disastrous so far. If you have any advice for me in that regard, I'd love to hear it."

"Hmm." Connor stroked his face, peering at me

thoughtfully for a moment. "I have a pretty good idea for keeping you out of trouble."

"Yeah?" I leaned forward across the table.

His smirk returned, and butterflies fluttered inside me.

"Do an exclusive act with me."

MELODY

"Say what, now?"

"Join my act, exclusively," Connor repeated. "Exclusive means you work only with me."

"I know what exclusive means," I hissed at his teasing grin. "Doing what, exactly?"

"Performing with me, in a strictly professional sense." He turned serious. "I'll split earnings with you right down the middle. And once everyone knows, no one will bother you. I have a reputation of being somewhat of an asshole." His grin returned as if proud of that notion.

"But performing how?" I demanded. "I can't walk in stilts, I can barely make it across the grounds in those heels they give me. I definitely can't do the crazy shit that you do."

I suddenly wondered how Connor was able to walk in stilts with no feet, especially as well as he did. It seemed like it would be extraordinarily difficult to control those long pieces of wood with half the leg muscles.

"To the audience, you'll look like you're just walking

across the stage, looking pretty and following my lead," he said. "But it will be a highly coordinated, choreographed routine. All you have to do is memorize the steps I teach you and keep time with the music."

Wait, he thought I was pretty?

"Okay." I rubbed my cheek like I was thinking, but really I was trying to hide my blush. "I think I can handle that. How long do I have to learn?"

Connor glanced at the clock above his kitchen sink. "About six hours."

"What?!" My eyes nearly popped out of my skull.

"I need you tonight," he said, looking somewhat apologetic. "Our fucking overlords have been wanting us to step up our shows each night." He rolled his eyes. "Something about building up hype for the wolf man display on the very last night of the carnival."

"Oh, yeah." I recalled the ringmaster's speech on the first night. "What's the deal with that?"

"Crock of shit," he scoffed. "Here's a tip for you, Mel—carnivals are scams. When everyone figures out the wolf man is bullshit and demands their money back, the company will still turn a profit because they crack the whip on us legitimate performers to jump higher and higher every night."

"Well, that's shitty," I frowned.

"It's reality." He shrugged, then his forest green eyes turned large and puppy-like. "So how 'bout it, Mel? Will you do this show with me?"

"Can I really learn the routine in six hours?" I gulped.

"I'm sure you can, babe." Just the way he said that made me swell up with confidence. "You're definitely smarter than the average chick here. We just have to repeat it a bunch of times so you have it down to muscle memory."

I thought about it for a few more moments and figured I had nothing to lose. I barely knew this guy, and yet I trusted him a hundred times more than Syko. With my whole heart, I believed he wouldn't try anything inappropriate, at least.

"Okay then," I stood from the table. "Guess we better get started."

❧

"Seriously?" I huffed. "You didn't tell me a hiking trip was part of this lesson."

Connor, about ten paces ahead of me, tossed a large water bottle over his head. I caught it after a bit of awkward juggling and sucked down greedily while trying to keep up with him. Not that I could get too close anyway due to his practice stilts—long, slender pieces of woods slung over his shoulder. They almost whacked me in the head a few times already.

"I like my privacy when I practice," was his reply.

The carnival grounds were well out of sight. I couldn't even see the Ferris wheel behind me anymore. Connor had been leading me through a nearby wooded area that turned into a straight up forest after about a mile. After yet another mile, he showed no signs of slowing down. For a man with no lower legs, he knew how to hustle down a barely-marked trail.

I had to admit, the view of his ass made the trek just a

bit more bearable. Not even the long, baggy pants he wore as part of his stilt walking getup could hide it.

"We're here," he said finally. He stopped so abruptly, I nearly got poked in the eye with his stilt again.

We came to a clearing where the grass was so short and jagged, it looked like a desert compared to the forest we just hiked through. The ground was dry and rock hard, with little water or vegetation to be seen.

"The deer population is out of control here," Connor said as he sat down on a tree stump. "They eat all the newly-grown vegetation. Sucks for the environment, but at least the ground is hard and flat. Good to practice on."

"They need natural predators," I whispered, primarily to myself. "Like wolves."

"Hey." Connor threw a small pebble at me. "You alright, Mel?"

"Yeah." I shook my head and blinked a few times. "That was weird. I spaced out for a second."

"You might be dehydrated. It's hot as Satan's balls out here," Connor smirked. "Chill out for a bit while I get ready."

I sat on a nearby tree stump and watched curiously as Connor rolled up his pant legs in preparation to put his stilts on. Right away, I saw exactly how he was able to pull off his stunts and my jaw nearly dropped.

His thighs were massive and looked to be made of pure muscle. The thin, spindly trees surrounding us couldn't compare to those trunks. His quad muscles flexed with power as he carefully removed his prosthetics. His left leg ended just below the knee and the right ended slightly lower, about halfway down the shin which was mottled with scar tissue.

Realizing I was staring, I looked away abruptly. Then curiosity got the better of me and I looked again. As he secured the stilts on, I saw he used them in place of his prosthetic legs. After wrapping his lower legs in some kind of compression fabric, he slid them into harnesses built into the wooden stilts and secured himself in with straps and buckles. Until then, I didn't notice one stilt was longer than the other to balance where he was amputated.

Then he grabbed a nearby tree and—using the trunk and the branches—hauled himself up to standing. Just like that, he was suddenly twelve feet tall and walking with the grace of a feline predator.

"Damn it. Forgot to set the music," he said. "Mel, will you grab my phone out of my pack and find the song for me?"

I rummaged through his pack while he walked around and warmed up. When I located the phone, I tried to avoid reading the message displaying on the lock screen, but couldn't stop myself. It was from someone named Vicky and read, "Are you ever going to talk to me again?"

I unlocked the phone and went directly to his music, for once refusing to give in to my burning curiosity. Snooping through his messages was wrong, especially since we barely knew each other. It didn't matter that jealousy flared up. What right did I have to be jealous? And anyway, the message seemed to imply that Connor wasn't talking to this Vicky person.

Following Connor's instruction's, I picked his performance song and set it on repeat. Over the next few hours, we practiced the routine. Or more accurately, he yelled at me like a drill sergeant while I tried my best to follow his instructions. Some of which seemed to defy physics.

"Four, five, six, seven, eight, stop!" I froze and felt his stilt slide at an angle behind me. "Now sit down, Mel," he commanded. "Trust me, don't be scared."

"That's what you said last time when I almost fell off!"

"You won't fall if you do it right," he sighed. "Swing your legs under a bit and grip with the back of your knees. Keep your hands on either side of you for extra support."

I lowered myself carefully onto the narrow, wooden replacement for his leg, which didn't seem wide enough at all to hold me, and suddenly I was lifted in the air.

"Ahh!" I screamed in the moment there was nothing underneath me. I was falling to the ground!

Out of nowhere, strong arms caught me and held me against a broad, solid chest.

"See?" Connor tightened his grip around my waist. "You're safe."

I clung to his broad shoulders and unintentionally nuzzled my face into his neck, not wanting to see how far away I was from the ground.

"How do I get down?" I asked in a small voice.

"There's a silk rope attached to my pants," he explained. "It's rolled up now. Unroll it and brace your feet against my legs as you go down, like you're rappelling down a rock wall."

"I've never rappelled down a rock wall in my life," I grumbled, fumbling around him for this so-called rope.

At twelve feet in the air with a definite chance of broken bones if he let go of me, I was still acutely aware of his massive arm around my waist. The way his muscles bunched and flexed from holding me and keeping his balance at the same time. A bead of sweat fell into the space between his collarbones and I had half a mind to lick it.

"It's behind me," he said in regards to my fumbling for the rope.

"Of course it is," I muttered. Right above his ass.

"Don't worry, it'll hold you. You can wrap it around yourself if it'll make you feel secure."

"You're the only thing making me feel secure." I bit my tongue too late. Those words had more of an implication than I intended.

If Connor noticed, he didn't let it on. "Put your feet against my leg," he said patiently. "And hold onto the rope until it's taut. You won't pull me with you."

I did as he instructed, and screamed when he removed his arm from around me.

"Stay there!" he instructed. A grin spread on his face as his arms spread out to the sides. "See? You're fine, babe."

"It hurts," I hissed through gritted teeth. Despite the softness of the silk, I gripped so hard it was digging into my hand. I braced myself against the side of his leg and held on the rope for dear life. If I allowed slack at either points, I'd go tumbling to the ground.

"Jump straight back, push with your legs," Connor instructed. "Let the rope slide through your hand for a bit before you clamp tight again. You'll swing back and be lower to the ground. Keep doing that until you hit the bottom."

"What happened to just walking back and forth across the stage?!" I demanded.

"That's most of what you'll be doing, but this is for the grand finale," he said. "I won't let you fall. You can do this, Mel. I know you can."

Amazing how another person's faith in me could give just the courage I needed. I repeated his instructions step-by-step in my head and took a deep breath. Bending my knees deeply, I sprang off and let the rope slide through my fingers for just a split second. Then my fear got the better of me and I grabbed it again. Connor's stilts came rushing back at me and I touched my feet to the side of them again.

"You did it!" Connor clapped his hands and his voice beamed with genuine pride.

I looked up and saw he was much further away than a split second ago. My feet were firmly planted against the wood of his stilt about six feet up from the ground.

"I really did it!" I shrieked with a mixture of bewilderment and glee.

The adrenaline rush hit me right then like a drug, making me feel invincible. I rappelled the rest of the way down in two easy jumps, landing lightly on my feet and spreading my arms in a *ta-da* pose.

"Great job, Mel!" Connor praised me from high above, and my heart swelled. "Now let's do it again. We've got to make it look pretty and shit."

The sun began sinking low over the trees as we went through the routine dozens of times. By the time Connor called it good, my arms screamed with fatigue and my legs felt like jello.

"Now we've got to do all that on stage?" I panted, sitting on the tree stump.

"Yep, for one last time." Connor secured his regular prosthetics on the stump next to me. "But you know it now. Once we're cleaned up and ready, our muscles will have enough rest to give it our all. It'll be a piece of cake, babe."

I hoped he was right, but not just about our performance. Getting anywhere near Syko again had my defenses on high alert. I hoped Connor was right about no one bothering me now that I was partnered with him.

Nothing was certain until showtime tonight.

13

MELODY

I applied my makeup carefully in the small bathroom of Connor's trailer. After picking out an outfit in the dressing tent, I got enough dirty looks from the other girls that I opted to make myself scarce. Apparently, Leeann and her friend did plenty more shit-talking about me.

"Almost ready, Mel?"

In the mirror, I saw Connor's eyes linger on me with an intense, heated gaze before turning away.

"Yep." I smacked my lips together after a final swipe of lipstick and thoroughly checked myself over.

I was able to find a short, pinstriped dress in the dressing tent that acted like a corset but provided more freedom to breathe. My waist nipped in nicely and my tits looked bodacious, but not overly pushed up into my face. Lacey black gloves and matching tights fit snugly over my hands and legs. An elaborate black beaded choker decorated my throat, and of course, the whole ensemble wasn't complete without a top hat.

A hum of excitement filled me as I was getting ready. Already, this felt different from the first night. Having Connor as a partner made me feel two-thousand percent more comfortable than being around Syko.

During practice, he was tough but encouraging. The only times he touched me was when it was necessary during our routine, and never for longer than was appropriate. I did catch him stealing glances at me like in the mirror just now, but those looks made my stomach flutter rather than fill me with dread.

"Ready when you are," I called, stalking slowly out of the bathroom on my tall heels.

He leaned against the counter, dressed in one of his many colorful suits for the show. Tonight, his dominant colors were purple and orange with accents of black. If I had a pop of orange in my outfit, we would have coordinated perfectly.

"Damn," he muttered under his breath. His green eyes lit up like orbs against the dark kohl surrounding them. It was the only makeup he wore, as he'd be wearing a black and purple mask during the show. I had to admit it looked sexy on him. With his bright clothes, he kind of resembled an eccentric pirate.

"What? Is it too much?" I asked, looking down at myself.

"No, not at all. You look great." His voice was low and husky as he jerked his eyes up and gave me a smile that almost seemed shy. "Shall we?"

He held out his elbow like a gentleman, which I accepted, wrapping my fingers underneath and around his massive bicep. We left the trailer arm in arm and headed toward the main stage.

Crickets came out and sang their song and the evening was illuminated by all the rides and carnival lights. Attendees, staff and performers all milled about, preparing for the nighttime events and we got several curious looks our way. I felt Connor stiffen next to me. He seemed to hate unwanted attention.

I lifted my chin and lengthened my steps, exuding my pride at walking next to him. As far as I cared, he was the only decent person at this carnival. With a light squeeze to his arm, I decided to tell him what was on the tip of my tongue since we left the trailer.

"You look great too, you know."

His bicep jumped underneath my fingers as if startled. He cast a sideways glance at me with that shy smile of his.

"Thanks, babe."

I felt him relax next to me, and then the fingers of his opposite hand curling around mine.

THE BACKSTAGE AREA WAS CHAOS. We were not the only act who had to step it up for the final night, it seemed. Everyone was doing last-minute practice sessions from juggling to fire breathing to sword swallowing.

Connor calmly secured his stage stilts as the ringmaster took to the stage and began his opening announcements.

"Ladies and gentlemen, boys and girls!" he boomed. "So good to see so many familiar faces! We've got a hell of a show for you tonight, unlike anything you've seen in the past week!"

"Yo, is this wolf man shit real or fake?" someone yelled

from the crowd. From where I sat, I could see an arm holding up a piece of paper. It was a carnival flyer with a cartoonish depiction of a werewolf printed on it.

"Ah, I'm so glad you asked, my friend!" the ringmaster answered theatrically. "The Wolf Man is most certainly real and a fearsome sight to behold! You may want to leave your young children at home tomorrow night, or risk nightmares of being eaten by the big bad wolf!"

He went on in dramatic fashion, avoiding more specific questions about the wolf man by urging people to attend tomorrow and see for themselves.

"Are we still all performing tomorrow?" I asked Connor.

"Nope," he answered dryly. "The wolf man scam is the only show. I hear tomorrow's tickets are almost sold out already," he added with disdain.

"Do we have to buy tickets too?"

"Nah, performers can see it for free." He cocked an eyebrow. "Don't tell me you're falling for this shit too, Mel."

"I just want to see the scam for myself," I said. "To satisfy my own curiosity."

"That's how they getcha," he chuckled, poking me playfully in the ribs. "Fine. But afterward, I get to take you on a romantic Ferris wheel ride."

Butterflies filled my entire torso to the point where even my breathing fluttered. I tried to minimize my smile as I said, "Sure, that sounds good."

The ringmaster finished talking, and our music cued up. The fluttering turned to sinking stones in my stomach and my heart threatened to beat out of my chest. Connor used the stage support to pull himself up to full, stilted height, but not before he dropped an affectionate peck to my cheek.

"You got this, babe." He winked down at me and slid on his mask. "Remember, just like we practiced."

I nodded, swallowed the lump in my throat, and steeled myself at the stage entrance. Connor strode out right on his cue. I counted carefully in my head and stepped out on my mark. If Syko taught me anything useful, it was the importance of smiling and waving. But this time, my smile felt genuine instead of plastered on. It only took a minute into our routine to realize that I was having fun.

The audience's faces were priceless as I weaved in and out of Connor's stilts across the stage. The moment it looked like he was going to step on or kick me, I did a little twirl or sidestep to show we were perfectly in sync. He walked on his hands for a minute, then touched his stilts down right in front of me in a crazy backbend. I did a dramatic pout and foot stomp when the stilts blocked my way and the crowd ate it up. I walked casually underneath his stilts as he elaborately crossed and uncrossed his legs in a crazy, tap dance sort of routine.

It went off flawlessly, and I couldn't believe how much fun I was having. Before I knew it, we were approaching the grand finale.

Connor got into position, angling his stilt like a lopsided bench, and I took a seat. Our eyes met for half a moment before he lifted his leg, tossing me through the air. I could only imagine the incredible amount of strength in his quads for him to pull that off.

Gasps and screams rose up from the crowd, now so far below me. For the briefest snapshot in time, I saw the

Ferris wheel and all the carnival lights on the horizon. It was a breathtaking view, and then I was falling.

Connor caught me with ease, securing an arm around my waist and holding me snugly against him. The music ended, and we held our free arms out to the sides in our final pose. The audience went absolutely nuts, cheering and throwing fists and hats in the air.

"Holy shit," I hissed, keeping my smile on as I looked out at everyone pressing in to get closer.

"Great job, babe," Connor said with a squeeze around my waist. His voice was muffled under the mask. "You were perfect. And not only that, they're nuts about you."

I couldn't pinpoint the emotion in his voice but from the corner of my eye, I saw the stage director motioning for us to get off for the next act. I rappelled down the silk rope tied to Connor's pants, and we did a final bow before taking our leave. The reactions backstage were mixed. Some congratulated us, others seemed annoyed that the opening act came out of the gate so strongly, like we showed up everyone else.

But we didn't care. We were riding high off the crowd's energy and how seamlessly we performed. Connor wore his biggest smile I'd seen yet as he ripped off his mask and we hurried away from the chaos so he could take the stilts off privately.

I was talking a mile a minute, feeling absolutely giddy at what we just accomplished. His energy was calmer than mine, more subdued as he put his legs back on, but I could feel the rush of excitement coming off him, too.

When he stood up and looked at me with such pride and warmth, I acted without thinking.

I wrapped my arms around his neck and kissed him.

14

CONNOR

Mel's lips tasted so sweet and my body felt so starved for a physical connection, I acted without thinking.

I pulled her tight against me and opened my mouth to hers. She let me in, sighing beautifully as her soft tongue grazed across my lips. Only when her short nails raked through my hair, did I come to the rest of my senses—and my brain panicked.

"Mel, stop." I pulled away, took a step back to put space between us, and immediately regretted it.

Her big doe eyes looked up at me with confusion and hurt. It was all I could do to not kiss that pain away again.

"Sorry," she mumbled quickly, removing her arms from around my neck and stepping back. "That was... really impulsive. I wasn't thinking at all. Just... forget it happened."

Those last words almost cut me as deeply as when Vicky left me for the last time. But over the years, I'd grown to not only accept it, but expect it. Women liked to tease and flirt with me, but once they found out my amputee status, I was baggage. A burden.

It didn't matter how much I flattered them or made them laugh, no one seriously wanted a guy who was missing a couple of limbs. No one wanted to sleep next to a partner who woke up screaming from nightmares.

"It's forgotten," I said with a tight smile, my chest aching painfully. "But we should still celebrate. Follow me, Mel."

We walked for a few minutes with some awkward distance between us. Damn it. Not even an hour ago, I felt on top of the world walking to the stage with her on my arm. Not only did she look damn gorgeous in her costume, she looked proud to be seen with me. No woman ever looked that happy to stand next to me since before my accident.

"Wait here," I told her, stopping just outside the booze tent. The two bitchy girls she worked with were still behind the bar, and I didn't want them giving her any shit.

I bypassed them, ignoring their dirty looks, and went straight to the back in search of Higgins. After a minute of sweet-talking, I convinced him to sell me an unopened bottle of champagne, already chilled. We were both veterans, so he tolerated me a bit more than most people.

Mel's eyes widened when I presented the bottle. "Where would you like to enjoy this?"

"How about on the grass where we can see the fireworks?" She pointed toward the sky, where the brightly colored bursts were already firing off.

Fuck.

I hated fireworks.

All the little hairs on my arms stood on end. My heart

began to speed up as my throat tightened. Usually I remembered when they were going off and planned accordingly, but Mel had me all distracted lately.

"Nah, let's go inside."

I hurried in the direction of my trailer, not waiting to see if Mel would catch up. The *boom-boom-crackle* of explosives sent my lungs tightening. I tried to keep my breaths deep and even, tried to remember when and where I was. I was *here*. Not back *there*.

"Connor, are you okay?"

She was somewhere behind me, or maybe right next to me. I couldn't be sure. All I knew was I had to get home and get my noise-canceling headphones on before I lost it.

Shit, I hadn't had a flashback in nearly a month. I had been doing so well. Every time I did have one, it felt like I regressed further back. Five steps forward, ten steps back.

I yanked open my trailer door and jumped in, not bothering to see where Mel was. I couldn't worry about her right now.

That was just another aspect that I hated. I was trained to protect those around me. It was my duty, my purpose. When my flashbacks came on like this, I had to abandon everything to focus on myself. It was pathetic. Ordinary people could watch fireworks with no issues, but I had to stop everything just to make sure I survived the next few minutes until it passed.

I found my headphones and stuck them over my ears. Just feeling the familiar pressure and the barrier between my brain and the outside world comforted me a bit. I sat on the edge of the bed and did my breathing exercises like I was taught by my therapist, just waiting it out.

I didn't notice my hands shaking until Mel's tiny,

slender fingers wrapped around them. Damn, she was still here? Why? And why did she kiss me? Did that really happen?

Real life and the flashbacks all seemed to blur together. My instinct was to shut my eyes tight, but I forced them open. I looked around, trying to take mental notes of my surroundings. I was *here*. Not back *there*.

Mel's long, slender legs in those sexy black tights stretched out next to mine, crossed at the ankles. I thought I could feel her lips on my shoulder, gently moving like butterfly wings. Was she saying something?

Eventually, the tightness in my chest faded. My pulse returned to normal and my lungs no longer felt like they were collapsing. I pulled off the headphones and let out a resigned sigh. That was exhausting. I could feel the weight of Mel's expectant gaze on me, but couldn't bring myself to look at her.

"Sorry about that," I muttered, wondering how best to explain my behavior. But my brain felt like scrambled eggs after what just happened.

"You have PTSD."

She said it matter-of-factly, but with a gentleness that showed she wasn't upset.

"Yes," I sighed. No point in lying to her. At this point, she knew more about me than all the people I met within the last three years.

Her fingers squeezed around mine gently. "Do you need anything?"

"Just a drink."

She removed her hand from mine and felt like she moved off the bed. My surroundings were still filtering in slowly, like I was coming out of a deep sleep.

I heard a *POP* that made me jump and then Mel's voice, "Sorry! I'm just opening the champagne."

In the next moment, my hands wrapped around a cold bottle, which I brought to my lips. Bubbles and a crisp, refreshing taste coated my throat. I passed the bottle toward Mel, but she held up a hand and shook her head in refusal.

She didn't want to drink. In that moment, I couldn't be concerned with why. All the better to numb myself with. After sucking down a fourth of the bottle, I allowed myself to look at her for the first time.

Her top hat was gone, but she still looked poised, perfect and elegant, sitting on the edge of my bed with her legs crossed.

"You don't have to stay with me," I muttered. "I'm good now."

"Hah. Where the hell would I go, Connor?" she scoffed. "Who else would I be with? After everything we did today?" Her hand closed around mine again. "I'm good right here, too."

Damn it. Not that I really wanted to be alone, but this girl was a whole new level of stubborn.

"What's it gonna take, girl?" I laughed bitterly. "Every day you spend with me, you learn more about how fucked up I am. How bad do I have to be before you finally run away screaming?"

"Syko bad," she answered quickly. "Which you're not and you never will be. I already know that."

I sighed wearily and leaned my head back, finally allowing my eyes to close. Every moment with this girl seemed to crack open my closed-off heart more and more. The longer she stuck around, the worse it would hurt later.

I already couldn't keep my eyes off her. After our grueling practice today, I found it increasingly difficult to keep my hands off her too.

"You know what? Fuck it." Mel took the bottle from me, set it on the ground and turned to face me. "I take it back. I'm *not* sorry." Before I could respond, the sweet, fruity taste of her lips were on mine again.

"Mel..." I tried to break away, but she kept leaning into me. "You don't—"

"I *do*, Connor," she insisted. "I want this. I wanted it earlier, but I chickened out. It's just been such a good day and you're... good to me. I don't care about the other stuff."

I shouldn't have given in. Fuck, she was so young and probably expecting too much—more than I could give—from this kiss.

But she was also an adult. Not only consenting, but wanting. And goddamn, she tasted so sweet.

I allowed my arms to go around her, and her tiny hands skimmed over my pounding heart. She pressed another kiss to me, shyly this time, and I accepted.

A light moan escaped her throat as I flicked her top lip with my tongue. We opened up to each other slowly, exploring with caution and hesitancy. Intrinsically, we knew the other person had boundaries, hangups, issues. We had seen glimpses of each other's inner demons and proceeded with slowness and gentleness, lest we uncover something not yet ready to be revealed.

I felt myself turning to putty from the inside out. How long had it been since I held a woman like this, kissing her for the first time?

I cradled Mel like a fragile bird in my arms as her soft

lips traveled across my face and neck like gentle rain. My hands began to grow exploratory too, running from her back to her waist, then her thighs.

Immediately, her energy shifted. She stiffened in my arms and her lips broke away from me.

"I don't want to, um, lead you on," she stammered. "Maybe I'll be ready to do more later, but I'm still kind of freaked out by, um—"

"Shh. It's alright, babe." I peppered her face with kisses. "We don't have to do anything you don't want to."

Her doe-eyed gaze filled my vision. "You're seriously okay with just kissing like teenagers?"

"You *are* a teenager," I teased.

She wrinkled her nose at me. "Not for that much longer."

"Even so," I chuckled. "Nothing will happen that you don't actively want to happen."

"Thank you," she sighed, seemingly with relief. "I'm just still shaken up by Syko touching me like that. I think I should take it slow for a bit."

Surprise filled me, but I made sure not to let it show on my face. I thought she had been freaked out by *me*. My legs, my flashbacks, or any other instance of moodiness I displayed. But none of that seemed to bother her.

No, it was that scumbag who still had a hold on her mind, making her scared to be physical with anyone else. I didn't mind that she just wanted to kiss, it was the most action I'd gotten in years. It just pissed me off that he made her feel this way and didn't give a shit about it.

I brought my hands back up to her arms, brushing light kisses across her eyelids and cheeks. Her thick, dark lashes fluttered against my lips, and she stifled a yawn.

"Do you want to lie down?" I asked.

She nodded. "It's been a long day."

Together, we slowly laid back on my mattress. Her head rested on my chest as she snuggled into my side, relaxed and fearless once again.

"Is it okay if I stay?" she asked softly after a few moments of cozy, blissful silence.

"Of course it is." I tightened my arm around her waist. My heart felt like it was leaping out of my chest with joy. But what goes up must always come down. "You can hit the light switch there."

She flicked the switch above her, and darkness surrounded us.

"I haven't felt like this in so long," she murmured sleepily.

"What's that?" I asked, almost fearing the answer.

"Safe."

MELODY

I woke up to solidness and warmth against my back. A heavy arm draped across me. For a moment, I forgot where I was and panicked. I shifted against the body behind me and the arm tightened around me. Fear held my breath until I looked down and saw I still had yesterday's clothes on. Not only that, my bedmate was still dressed too.

Relief swept over me as a smile came to my lips. Connor showed a really sweet, tender side of himself last night. His flashback was scary to witness, and I felt like shit for wanting to bring him out to the fireworks. The moment I saw that panicked look in his eye, I should have known.

He stirred next to me with a groan, and his arm lifted off me to rub his face. I took the opportunity to sit up and stretch.

"Making your escape already?" he asked groggily.

"No," I answered. "Just... waking up."

"Mm." He shifted, groaned, and stretched. Damn it, why did he have to be so nice to look at? "You okay?"

"Yeah," I answered, a smile playing at my lips. "I just... didn't expect to sleep so well."

"Oh, yeah?" He folded his arms behind his head, making his biceps flex. "Having regrets?"

My brow furrowed. "About what?"

"You know," he said softly. "Dealing with my shitty mental illness. Staying the night in this four-wheeled piece of shit. Kissing me."

I didn't know how to tell him a *no* that was strong enough. After everything he did for me, this guy was still convinced I wanted to walk away? So I leaned over him and smashed my mouth down on his.

He let out a groan of surprise, then chuckled against my lips before kissing me back. Just like last night, he was gentle and explorative. His arms wrapped around my back and, aside from caressing my face, strayed nowhere else. The more he held back and respected my boundaries, the more my body yearned to feel him push them. But I took comfort in knowing he wouldn't, not until I wanted him to.

"Your PTSD is not your fault," I told him. "None of this is. And I can't stop myself from kissing you, but you gotta kiss me first sometime too."

He chuckled and obliged, lifting his head up to kiss me deeply. I felt it in pleasant tingles from my lips all the way down to my toes. I'd kissed plenty of boys at school before, but never a *man*. Every touch and taste from him carried the confidence of experience. We barely knew each other, but he seemed to know exactly what my body needed. And still he stopped himself, never testing to see what he could get away with like those awkward, fumbling teenage boys.

"Why are you still here, Mel?" he asked, tracing his fingertips down my arms. "Why did you stay last night?" He didn't sound annoyed, but genuinely curious to know.

"Because I wanted to," I answered.

"But why?" The forest of his eyes made me lose sense of everything outside them. "You don't need to drag yourself down with me. You're young, gorgeous, able-bodied. Your mind isn't as... damaged as mine."

"Stop," I told him sternly. "I stayed because you shouldn't be alone when you're going through that. You looked out for me, so the least I can do is be here for you."

He sighed, leaning back on his pillow. "What are you looking for, though? I mean, what do you want out of life? I have my good qualities, but God knows I'm flawed as fuck, too. I'll never be able to watch fireworks with you. I have a temper and I'll probably hurt your feelings. I'll probably never have enough money to buy you nice things. And that doesn't even touch on the fact that I'm missing limbs and just can't do certain things."

"I don't need any of that," I insisted. "And I don't care what your flaws are. We all have them. I do too."

"You should have higher standards," he laughed, brushing my hair out of my eyes.

"Like what?" I demanded. "A rich guy who'll buy me useless shit but won't take care of me when I'm throwing up on myself? Or someone with all their limbs but treats women like Syko does?"

"You'll have more choices than that," he argued. "You can have literally anyone you want without settling."

"I'm not settling," I retorted. "I want *you*, Connor. I

don't know where I'll be in five or ten years or even next week, but I'm sure I want you right now."

He sighed and didn't say anything for the longest time. For a moment, I wondered if I misinterpreted everything. Was he trying to talk me out of being with him because he didn't want *me*?

But then he broke out into a smile that lit up his handsome face. "I kept telling myself you're too good to be true. But good things rarely come my way, so I'll keep you as long as you can stand to have me."

Relief swept over me like a wave. Then lightness and joy bubbled up within me like a well. Finally, I felt like I could trust someone. Like I could relax and be myself. My life no longer revolved around me taking care of others. We could support each other.

Who knew how long it would last? Maybe it was unwise of me, but I never thought that far ahead. Even if he turned around and became a monster tomorrow, I wouldn't regret knowing him in the short time I did.

At some point, I got up and made us coffee, but we spent most of the day in bed. Hours felt like minutes as we talked, laughed, and kissed. I couldn't remember a time where I felt so at ease and relaxed. Before we knew it, the sun cast long shadows as it dipped low on the horizon.

"Damn, where did the day go?" I leaned back against Connor's chest as the sky began turning a golden pink.

"It's great to have a day off," he murmured, dropping a kiss to my shoulder. "I still owe you a romantic Ferris wheel ride."

"Damn right you do." I nuzzled his face. "Oh! That means the Wolf Man show is tonight, right?"

"Yeah." He pulled away to look at me, amusement dancing in his eyes. "You still want to go?"

I nodded. "Ferris wheel before or after?"

"Let's do it after." His lips brushed against mine sensually. "So when you're inevitably disappointed by the sham, I can still impress you with my thoughtfulness and charm."

"You already do."

He looked genuinely taken aback and confused before that infectious smile lit up his handsome face. I had a feeling no one told him that in a long time.

"Let me grab a set of clothes," I said, rising reluctantly from the bed. "And I'll be right back."

"Hurry back," he said, clasping my hands for the longest moment he could. "I have a feeling I'll miss you already."

16

MELODY

The crowd was so thick, I had to clamp down tightly onto Connor's hand to avoid losing him. Bodies pressed in all around as we slithered our way through. I caught bits and pieces of conversation as we passed people.

"What do you think the Wolf Man really is?"

"Probably just a fucking dog they taught to stand on two legs."

"I bet it is just a really hairy dude. I really want to know, though..."

"Fuckin' triple the cost of regular admission? It better be a real fuckin' werewolf."

We reached a spot near the right side of the stage, right up against the gate. Stern-looking security guards stood just on the other side of the gate beneath the stage. Their eyes traveled sharply across the crowd pressing in as close as they could to the barrier.

"They're armed," Connor muttered, his eyes falling to

the holstered pistols at the guards' hips. "Something's fishy about this."

I swallowed and took a deep breath, but nothing seemed to calm my nerves. For some inexplicable reason, I had to see this, and not for the novelty or morbid curiosity that drove everyone else here. Something in my body pulled me to this spot, like my soul was on a chain being yanked here for a reason I didn't know yet.

The drums started up in time with my hammering heartbeat and the spotlights focused on the red stage curtain. Whistles and cheers rose up from the audience, followed by chants of, "Wolf man! Wolf man! Wolf man!"

The ringmaster entered from the opposite side of the stage from us, taking his place in the center.

"Ladies and gentlemen, boys and girls!" his voice boomed. "I'm so pleased you could join us tonight for our ultimate show here in lovely Drowningville. As promised, we've saved the best for last!"

"Better be worth it!" someone called out.

"Absolutely, my good man!" The ringmaster declared. "This isn't a freak show like the days of the past, with gimmicks and scams, oh no! Behind this curtain is something that, by all the laws of nature and God, should absolutely not exist."

Connor's arm slid around my waist protectively. I didn't even realize how tense I was until he rubbed my back. Squeezing his fingers, I leaned back against his chest and pressed a kiss to the closest spot I could reach, just under his chin.

"To be honest with you good folks," the ringmaster continued. "We shouldn't even be showing you this beast. The moment we captured it, we should have contacted the government. But who are we to deny what the people want?"

"Just show us already!" someone shouted.

"The second we're in danger, I'm getting us out of here," Connor growled into my ear. "I don't have a good feeling about this at all, babe."

"Me neither," I admitted. "But I have to see."

The ringmaster waved his white-gloved hand, and the curtains pulled back to the sound of thunderous applause. Onstage, a red sheet draped over a tall rectangular structure, which I could only assume was a cage. As if on cue, the security detail gathered closer to the stage, their hands resting on the weapons at their hips.

"Remember this is a once in a lifetime opportunity, folks." The ringmaster walked in a slow circle around the cage and picked up an electric cattle prod from a nearby table. "We've taken all the precautions possible, but still don't know the full strength and abilities of this beast. We made you sign waivers with your ticket purchases because we cannot guarantee your safety."

He stuck the cattle prod to the side of the covered cage and pulled the trigger.

An ear-piercing howl, followed by violent rattling and a monstrous roar unlike anything I'd ever heard, rang out into the night. With a collective gasp, the whole crowd seemed to flinch and back away as one entity. Connor held me tightly against his chest.

"What the fuck..." he mumbled.

Everyone else had a similar reaction. The heckling quieted down to a low, cautious murmur. Faces went from curious and jovial to serious, with a healthy dose of fear.

"I warned you, folks!" The ringmaster held up the

cattle prod like a beacon. Whatever was inside the cage made low huffing and growling noises. "If you cannot handle looking straight into the face of Hell, I suggest you walk away now! This is truly unlike anything you have ever seen, or ever will see again!"

"Show us!" one person shouted, apparently gaining their courage back swiftly. Others quickly echoed their agreement.

Realizing he couldn't tease and titillate the thirsty audience any longer, the ringmaster took a handful of the cloth in his fist.

"Ladies and gentlemen, boys and girls! I give you," he paused dramatically, "the Wolf Man!"

He yanked the cloth down over the cage with a flourish, revealing the beast within.

A choked gasp escaped my chest, and I lifted my hands to my mouth, but not because of fear or disgust. My eyes immediately began welling with tears for the poor caged creature onstage.

The poor thing was so tall and broad, he could barely turn around in the cramped prison. He did look like a wolf standing on two legs, with hands and feet that looked somewhat like paws. The lower half of his face extended out slightly like a snout, with a long tongue that lolled out as he panted and revealed rows of glistening, pointed teeth. He was covered from head to toe in beautiful silvery-white fur, and his golden eyes were dilated and unfocused.

"He's got to be drugged," I whispered to Connor, the tears spilling freely down my cheeks. "Oh my God, the poor thing. This is fucking awful."

"What... How?" Connor blinked as if he didn't register what I said, just stared at the stage in disbelief. "How's this even possible? That thing looks *real*."

"He is!" I cried. "And look at how they're treating him!"

The ringmaster prodded the beast again with a jolt of electricity, sending him snarling, growling, and pressing against the metal bars to get away. I only then noticed all the bruises and burn marks on his ribs. The audience roared, hooting and hollering and jamming in closer to get a better look. Some were already trying to climb over the barricade and were immediately stopped by security.

"I see some of you are still skeptical!" the ringmaster yelled over the cacophony of voices. "I don't blame you, of course! But fortunately, we have further proof to the validity of the Wolf Man! If you still feel this is a hoax, then how would you like to meet," he paused, waiting for the crowd to quiet down, "the Wolf Man's *children?*"

"Oh, no..." My heart seemed to stop in my chest. "Please don't tell me..."

The wolf-man's semi-human ears pricked forward. His head jerked in the direction of the ringmaster, indicating he understood perfectly what was said.

A stagehand brought out a smaller cage, about the size of a regular dog crate, also covered with a cloth. The wolf-man pressed his face hard between his own bars, sniffing the air and making soft whimpering sounds.

"Oh my God, they can't be doing this," I whispered. Watching the scene play out before me was like watching my own heart break.

Standing between the two cages with his cattle prod

raised high in one hand, the ringmaster ripped the cloth off of the smaller cage with the other.

And the wolf man absolutely lost his shit.

He went berserk, was the most accurate way to describe it. He howled at the top of his lungs, yanked and pulled and pounded on the bars with all of his might, to no avail. His cage must have been bolted into the floor because it absolutely would not move.

And the audience laughed. They *laughed* at the distraught father trying to reach his children, two miniature versions of him huddled in the small cage, shaking and whimpering with their ears flattened against their skulls as they held each other. They looked to be about the human age of five or six years old, but also with canine features and covered in fur. The boy's fur was white like his dad's and the girl's was a beautiful pattern, ticked with gray, black, and brown.

"This is so fucked up," Connor said in disbelief. "Holy shit, they're just babies."

When the father realized he could not get to his children, he looked to the ringmaster, standing pompously just out of reach of his claws. The wolf man's jaws moved as yowls, yips, and barks came out. He was trying to speak, no doubt pleading for his children to be left alone.

And the sadistic fucker nodded, raising his eyebrows as if listening raptly to the caged man's pleas, which the audience found endlessly amusing.

"Ah, yes indeed. I see what you're saying," the ringmaster said mockingly before electrocuting him again.

The howls of pain that followed radiated through my eardrums and rattled my skull. I covered my ears and Connor pulled my head into his chest, but I didn't miss the pups' reaction and that was what severed my heart in two.

They let go of each other and ran to the edge of their cage, sticking their skinny arms out as far as they could, but to no avail. They yelped and whined and cried as they swiped in the direction of the ringmaster's shoes, trying desperately to stop the torture being inflicted on their father.

His painful howls eventually stopped, and the thump of flesh against metal bars indicated he was unconscious. The audience laughed uproariously, while I could only sob into Connor's shirt, clutching him tightly. The children's screaming continued. For all they knew, their father was just murdered as part of a performance.

"Let's go." Keeping my head tightly pressed to his heart, Connor turned us away and began shoving through the crowd. "We don't need to see this disgusting shit."

My feet followed limply, without protest. A cold numbness settled over my body, but there was no escaping what played on a repeating loop in my head. And the ache in my heart felt so deep that it tore through my soul.

Connor took us all the way back to his trailer, where he laid me down on the small bed and covered me with a blanket. I curled into a ball and just sobbed, my whole body wracking with deep, ragged breaths.

Hesitantly, Connor laid down behind me and draped a large, muscular arm over my waist. I tried to take small comfort in him being there, as he rubbed my arms and placed soft kisses on my shoulder. But then I remembered those two kids, scared and alone, as they watched their dad get mistreated with no one to help.

It made what Syko did to me look completely harmless in comparison.

"I'm sorry, babe," Connor murmured, planting a gentle kiss behind my ear. "People are terrible. I wish there was something we could do."

"There has to be." I flipped over to face him. "We can't do *nothing*. Those poor kids..." My voice was raw from crying and still fresh tears spilled.

"I know." He used the pad of his thumb to gently wipe my tears away. "Trust me, I wanted to murder that fucking ringmaster and every heartless asshole in the audience."

"We have to do something." I sat up abruptly, wiping my face and nose with a shaky breath. "I hate myself for every second I'm sitting here crying and they're the ones who are actually suffering."

"I get what you're feeling, babe. But how?" Connor reached out and squeezed my knee. "What can an old curmudgeon and an eighteen-year-old girl do for a... werewolf family or whatever the fuck they are?"

"I don't know yet." I hung my head in my hands.

"And here's another thing to think about," he went on. "Yes, they were being mistreated, and that's fucked up, but we still don't know *what* they are. What if they're dangerous? What if they love to eat humans? It's totally possible you want to help something that would turn around and kill you the first chance it got."

"That's not how they are." My voice grew steadier and my eyes drifted to the waning moon out the trailer window.

"Mel, how do you know that?"

My thoughts drifted back to the wolf man in his cage.

His golden eyes showed intelligence and depth. He under-stood what the ringmaster said and tried speaking to him. He didn't act like a wild animal, but a *person*. And the deepest part of my heart told me he was exactly that.

"I just know."

17

MELODY

The longer I laid there and allowed my thoughts to spiral, the more restless I became. Hours had gone by and the show was long over. If the wolf people were treated that badly in front of an audience, I didn't dare speculate how bad it was when no one was looking. Every passing second was another moment of those kids being terrified or hurt, and I couldn't stand to not do anything about it.

I tossed the blanket off me and stood from the bed. My fingers brushed against my lucky coin in my pocket for a dose of courage, then I started putting on my shoes and jacket.

"Where are you going?" Connor mumbled in the darkness.

"I'm helping the wolf family escape."

He sprang up, sliding his hand along the wall for the light switch. I pounced to stop him, straddling his waist and catching his wrists. I was nowhere near strong enough to actually stop him, but his movements paused and a low groan escaped his chest. He was rock hard beneath me and I felt my core hollow out in response. Our breath mingled for half a moment. As much as I wanted to explore this, now was not the right time.

"You can come or not," I whispered. "But I'm going and don't want anybody seeing."

"Melody." His voice was a mixture of threatening, arousal, and pleading. On an instinctual level, I wanted to hear him say my name like that again and again.

But again, not the right time. I had to focus.

"You'll get caught before you can reach them," he growled. "They've got to be heavily guarded. Who knows how many others want to help themselves to a closer look?"

"Then help me."

I released his hands and let my fingers travel up his massive arms to wrap around his shoulders. A sliver of moonlight came through the window and illuminated part of his face and one stunning green eye like a mask.

Honestly, I was scared shitless of doing this alone. He had a strange way of making me feel safer and more confident when he was at my side. Like a huge, disgruntled guardian angel, he had been looking out for me since my first day here.

And I was beginning to realize how much I wanted him at my side through everything, no matter where this crazy freak show of a life took us.

"Please, Connor." My fingers found his lips in the dark, brushing against the rough stubble on his jaw. "It's the right thing to do. You know it is."

"Fuck, Mel." His mouth captured mine savagely as his arms wrapped around me and crushed me against his chest. "You're going to get us in an assload of trouble. But the thing is, I know I won't regret a damn second of it."

My heart dared to leap with hope. "So you'll help me save them?"

"Get your sweet little ass off me." He patted my thigh. "Let me put my legs on."

Within minutes, we silently crept out the door and across the carnival grounds.

The attendees were gone, but some staff and performers were still out and winding down for the evening. The sounds of glasses clinking and multiple conversations drifted over from the booze tent, still open and lively. Others drank, smoked, and played cards in smaller, quiet circles on picnic tables. We headed in the general direction of the booze tent, and no one batted an eye.

Once out of sight, we took a hard left and walked as casually as we could behind the rows of tents and trailers. I realized vaguely this was where all the tools and equipment were stored for breaking down the Ferris wheel, booths, and everything else. It looked like a junkyard.

"This is the most likely spot they'll keep them," Connor whispered. "Out of sight, out of mind when surrounded by pieces of junk."

Before I could respond, he grabbed my arm and pulled me to duck behind the rusted shell of a car. He held a finger to his lips and looked at me insistently. I nodded and listened hard.

Voices and footsteps slowly approached, and we ducked further back, careful not to make a sound.

"Jesus, dog-sitting fucking sucks," one of the voices

complained. "I could be in the booze tent right now with a bottle of whiskey and a pair of tits in my face."

"I hear ya," the other voice commiserated.

"Say." The first voice perked up as if hit with a jolt of inspiration. "What if I grab a bottle and come right back? It'll make the time go faster."

"Yes, go," Connor mouthed silently, clenching his fists.

"I dunno, man." The second voice was hesitant. "Jenkins was hard up about keeping two of us on these mutts at all times, no matter what."

"Aw, come on, you pussy. They're out cold," the first voice protested. "It'll just take a second to sweet-talk the pretty bartender and swipe a bottle."

"I know how you get around female attention," his partner snarled. "First pair of titties you see and you have the memory of a goldfish. Next thing I know, I'm out here for another two fuckin' hours by myself."

Connor and I barely breathed as we listened and waited for them to finish arguing. Finally, the first guy got his permission to visit the booze tent. The second guy grumbled angrily as his partner pranced off and he headed back to his post. Connor wasted no time and jumped on him in the blink of an eye.

With nothing more than a quick thud and a grunt, the guard went down like a sack of potatoes.

"Holy shit!" I shrieked, almost forgetting to whisper. "What was that?"

"Just knocked him out." Connor flashed me a smile as he patted the guy down. "Marine corps, baby."

"How do you know he's not dead?"

"We've got no time to find out." Connor fished a set of

keys from the unconscious man's pocket and grabbed my hand. "Let's move before the other one comes back."

It didn't take long for us to find the wolf family. After only a minute, a flash of white fur caught my eye among the rusted metal and warped wooden boards of the junkyard. Connor and I made a beeline straight for them, and what I saw made me want to burst into tears again.

The children were in the same cage as before, curled up in each other's arms and appeared to be sleeping. The father had been moved to a shorter, wider cage where he couldn't stand up at all and could barely stretch out. He too appeared to be sleeping, though his breaths wheezed with labor through the crude muzzle they clamped over his snout. It looked like little more than a leather belt.

"Hey," I whispered, tapping on the bars of his cage. "We're here to let you out." He didn't move a muscle, so I tapped a little more insistently.

"We don't have time for this, babe," Connor murmured urgently.

"They must be sedated," I realized, looking up at him. "Connor, we're gonna have to drag them out of here."

His eyes widened. "What? How?"

"I'll take the kids. You carry him." I snatched the keys from his hand and proceeded to unlock the cages.

"Melody, stop!" he hissed, but I ignored him, opening the cage doors wide. He grabbed my wrists before I could do anything else and brought his face down close to mine. "Mel, what are we supposed to do with them?"

"We take them back to the trailer and hide them there."

Connor rubbed his face. I could tell his patience was wearing thin with me, but I was not about to let this family get abused again without a chance to escape or fight back. Consequences be damned.

"And then what?"

"Then we get the fuck out of here," I replied coolly. "It's the last night. We already got paid. Why bother to stick around?"

A heavy pause hung between us and for a moment, I wondered if he'd had enough. I waited for him to storm off and leave me to deal with them on my own, but he sighed and stuck his torso into the father's cage.

"I don't know why I keep going along with your crazy shit, girl," he grumbled as he began dragging the unconscious wolf man from his cage.

"'Cause you love me," I joked, reaching in and gently separating the children from each other.

Connor mumbled something in reply, but I didn't hear him over adjusting the boy's head on my shoulder before securing the girl on my other arm.

Their fur was incredibly soft with the fuzzy quality of a young puppy. Another stab went through my heart at the thought of how innocent they were, and how cruel it was to subject them to this.

With each child secured in my arms, I carefully pulled out of the cage and stood up, using all the strength in my legs. The kids sat like sandbags in each of my arms, each of them leaning limply against me like rag dolls. I wouldn't have the strength to carry them far.

Connor slung the wolf man's torso over his shoulders, carefully securing his arm and leg in a fireman carry, then stood to his full height with all the power and confidence of a bodybuilder. I only then realized how truly gigantic the wolf man was. Connor was broader and more muscular, but his prosthetics didn't make him much taller than me. The wolf man had to be at least six-foot four, made of long, lean muscles under his white fur. With how cramped those cages were, it was impossible to guess his full stature before now.

"Let's go."

Connor started off, and I followed him, keeping the kids as steady in my arms as possible. My heart crashed against my ribs and my eyes darted around for anyone being alerted to us. Running would draw too much attention, so we speedwalked through the alley behind all the tents and trailers, going behind trucks, port-a-potties, and more random storage and parts to avoid being seen.

A heavy ache settled into my arms, but spotting Connor's trailer up ahead put a renewed spring in my step. Not much farther!

Unfortunately, that was the moment the girl began waking up.

Still with her eyes closed, she squirmed in my arms, pushing away at my chest while making soft whimpering sounds.

"Shh, it's okay!" I whispered to her. "We're helping you. It's gonna be okay."

She spun around in my arms, clearly disoriented and trying to get her bearings. All I could do was keep her locked between my forearm and my chest while my feet kept moving and my other arm holding onto her brother. The poor thing must have opened her eyes and seen her dad draped across Connor's shoulders a few feet ahead, because right then she began howling bloody murder.

I pulled her face into my chest, trying as best I could

to cover her mouth. "I'm sorry. I'm really sorry, little one, but you have to be quiet."

"We've got to run," Connor hissed, picking up his pace. "Someone definitely heard that."

I willed my feet to move faster, gritting my teeth against my arms begging to fall off. Through the air whipping past my ears, I heard distant voices shouting, but didn't dare look back or slow down. My eyes stayed locked on Connor's back as my panic heightened. Then the boy, stronger and bigger than his sister, started wriggling in my fatigued arms.

"Stop, stop!" I pleaded. The boy struggled so hard, I was seconds away from dropping him. "Connor!"

"Shut up!" he snapped. He was at the door to his trailer and fumbling for his keys.

I came right up on his heels, every muscle burning from running and carrying these kids. The moment I stopped, the boy began slipping out of my grasp, kicking and clawing at my shins. In his mind, he was already so close to escape and feeling the ground so close to his feet spurred him on.

"Kid, listen to me!" I brought my mouth down close to his ear. "You will die or get captured if you run from me. If you want to escape, stop fighting!"

He stopped just long enough for Connor to throw open the door and rush inside. In a flash, Connor lowered the father to the floor and sprang up to the driver's seat. I followed, quickly spinning around and slamming the door shut behind me before finally relieving myself of the weight of two incredibly squirmy children.

I dragged in a shaky breath, leaning against the door,

but could not afford to relax yet. Connor already turned the vehicle on and started driving us out.

The pups ran with wobbly gaits to their still-unconscious father on the floor, nuzzling and pawing at him with soft whimpers. One of them yanked off his muzzle and his breathing seemed to grow deeper, his chest rising and falling rhythmically.

The floor swayed beneath my feet as Connor took a hard turn, then he hit the gas and sent me stumbling back toward the bed. The wolf family didn't seem to pay any mind. They were all alive and not trying to escape us yet, so I carefully moved up to the front.

Connor's shoulders bunched up and tensed near his ears. His handsome face was a scowl of concentration as he drove us like a bat out of hell off the carnival grounds.

"Can I help with anything?" I asked timidly, reaching for his shoulder.

"Get down," he barked. "Stay out of sight."

I did as he said, slinking down to the floor behind his seat and trying not to take his tone personally. Turning around, I saw the pups nestled under their father's arm. They were quiet and looked calmer, though still wary of us and their surroundings. The boy watched me with his wild, golden eyes. His lips curled back in a snarl to show me his baby wolf teeth in a warning.

I just nodded, not knowing how else to show I understood.

"We're getting far away from those bad people," I said. "You're not our prisoners. Once we're far away, you guys can go free."

The boy put his teeth away and his ears pricked forward. He did that cute puppy head-tilt as if pondering my words. Amidst all the chaos and adrenaline of this crazy day, I had to let myself smile. It was too adorable not to.

"Mel, babe." Connor's voice floated back to me, the harsh edge of it gone.

"Yeah?" I lifted my head up in his direction.

"Will you check the mirrors for me? See if anyone's behind us."

"Yeah."

I positioned myself out of sight behind his seat, but still within clear view of the mirrors. I relayed every headlight I saw as we made off like thieves in the night.

18

MELODY

We drove for what felt like hours in darkness and silence. Connor kept the headlights off as we put more and more distance between us and that awful carnival.

Are all of them like this? I wondered as we lumbered down the road. Did the carnival I attended as a child also treat its attractions this way? And its performers? Did every carnival have a sadistic, abusive ringmaster and a Syko in their midst?

The more I thought about it, the more it seemed like the outside world wasn't any rosier than the shitty trailer park I grew up in. For those like the wolf family, it was a hundred times worse. At least I was never treated like an animal growing up. I was treated like shit and taken advantage of, for sure. But I could never imagine going through what those three did.

No, the only good thing I had going for me was Connor, and even he seemed pissed off at me half the time. Oh, and the satisfaction of saving a family from more abuse and mistreatment, I guess.

I was still stewing in my thoughts when the vehicle slowed and finally took a complete stop. No headlights had shown up in the mirrors for the past two hours and it seemed Connor was finally ready to rest for the night.

"Should be safe here. I'll kick on the generator," he mumbled, brushing past me with barely a glance. He was careful however, to step around the wolf family still sprawled on the floor.

The father still showed no signs of consciousness. Whatever they gave him must have been a huge dose. His children looked fairly content though, sleeping peacefully and curled up against his thick fur. Who knew when they were all last able to snuggle up together? The sight tugged at my heartstrings as the inside lamps gently flickered on.

Connor walked slowly back through to collapse on the bed. He pulled up his pant legs, swiftly removed his prosthetics, then reclined back on the mattress with a heavy sigh.

After a moment, he lifted his head to look at me. "Whatchu doin' all the way over there?"

I lifted a shoulder in a lazy shrug. "I can never tell if you're mad at me or not," I admitted.

He propped himself up on his elbows and gave me a curious look. "Why would I be mad at you, babe?"

I flicked my eyes in the direction of the wolf family sleeping peacefully on the floor. He hadn't wanted to get involved, but I dragged him into it. My sense of justice was so overwhelming at times, I forgot that most people didn't feel the same way I did.

"Hey," he said softly and patted the space next to him. "Come here."

I rose to my feet and crawled across the mattress toward him, still feeling a little apprehensive. He drew me to his side and dropped a kiss to my head, knowing full well that would make me melt like putty in his arms.

"I was never mad at you, babe. The situation was just stressful and I get hyper-focused when shit like that happens. I go right back to being a soldier. A machine carrying out a mission."

"I didn't mean to take you back to that mindset," I said, chewing my lip over the guilt. It was bad enough that he had PTSD. How shitty was it of me to make him revert back to the worst period of his life?

Shit. Comparatively speaking, I was the one person in the trailer with the least to complain about.

"Not your fault, babe. That's just in my nature." He stroked my hair absentmindedly and got a faraway look in his eyes.

"What? To take command of a dangerous situation?" I propped my chin up on his chest to look at him.

"No." His gaze dropped. "To protect you."

My heart squeezed in my chest, an unfamiliar but not unwelcome feeling. Warmth and lightness spread throughout my limbs.

"Why?" I asked. No one else had ever felt the need to protect me. I was always the protector.

"Because," he paused for a moment, tightening his arm around me. "You remind me of what it was like to be happy."

The lightness and warmth in me spread all the way to

my toes, and I had the unbearable urge to smile and bury my face in his side. I felt comfortable and relaxed. Was this happiness?

"When I'm with you, I think I'm starting to figure out what that feels like," I said cautiously.

He tilted my chin up to look at him, surprise and concern in his green eyes.

"You don't know what being happy feels like?"

"Well, I know what it means," I mumbled, heat rising shamefully in my cheeks. "And I kind of remember the feeling. The closest thing to happiness was when I went to the carnival as a little kid. That's why I ran away and joined. I was clinging onto that."

He said nothing for a moment, just stroked my hair absently as we listened to the wolves snore a few feet away on the floor.

"It does suck, growing up and learning what you thought as a kid isn't true," he said gently. "Adulthood is full of disappointing shit, but to be jaded and bitter about it? That's a choice." He chuckled. "I should know. I'm probably the most jaded, bitter old bastard you'll ever meet."

"You have a right to be, though," I argued. "You almost died, and then your country took a shit on you when you came home. Then you ended up in this place where you have to hide your injuries or get treated like a freak." I nodded toward the wolves. "Like them."

"Sure, but then I met this adorable spitfire of a girl who pushes all my buttons, makes me laugh, and drags me along on dangerous rescue missions." He dropped a kiss to my lips that turned all of my bones to jello. "It's all about your perspective, babe."

"So you're not wishing you never met me right now?" I had to pry my eyes away as those words, my biggest insecurity at the moment, tumbled out of me.

"Hell no." He forced me to look at him again. "You know how long I worked in that shithole?"

I shook my head.

"Two years. Two years of my life being a goddamn tap-dancing monkey because my other option was begging on the street. I couldn't even tell you why I wanted to keep living another day. Then you came along and shook everything up. You gave me reasons to smile and punch Syko in his fucking teeth. You've turned my world upside down and I wouldn't have it any other way."

"Me neither," I sighed, settling into the warm glow that radiated from being near him, and from the knowledge that he didn't think of me as some annoying little kid. I wanted to hold on to this and never let it go.

"Tell me about when you were happy before," I said, allowing a hand to snake across his chest. "What was your life like back then?"

"Well, damn," he laughed softly. "Let me see, it's been so long."

He eased back onto the pillows, his arm still snug around my waist and allowing me to lay my head on his chest. The watery thud of his heartbeat greeted my cheek as we laid together and got comfortable.

"I was a typical guy in my twenties, I guess," he began. "Going to college, working part-time, partying on weekends and being a drunk idiot with my friends. Life was simpler back then. I was busy, but I just did everything I was supposed to do and was working toward a goal. I was always a country boy, but I wanted to work in finance. I wanted to wear a fancy suit, have a corner office, get away from the rednecks and all that corporate bullshit."

"What made you join the marines?" I asked.

"Um, well," he stammered a bit. "Turns out it's hard to get a competitive job in finance right after you graduate, especially for a small-town hick like me with no connections." He forced out a laugh. "And my girlfriend at the time wanted a ring and a stable future. She wanted me to prove I could step it up and support a family, so the military made the most logical sense."

The memory of seeing the text message on Connor's phone flashed through my mind. Was that who he was talking about?

"Yeah? What did she do to prove she could give *you* a stable future?" I said with more hostility than I intended. My jealousy was showing, but I didn't care.

"Easy, tiger," he chuckled, giving me a squeeze. "That's just how things are around these parts. The man is expected to provide, so that was what I signed up to do."

"And?" I pressed. "Did you prove your worth to her?"

"I did after I completed basic and finished my first tour," he mumbled. "I came home on leave, went straight to the jewelry store and bought the ring she wanted. She said yes and everything was great." He smiled sadly. "That was until I got back from my second tour as only half the man I used to be."

"Don't say that." I smacked his chest. "You're not any less of a man."

"It's a joke, babe." He mussed up my hair playfully. "I don't take my leg situation too seriously anymore, so you don't have to, either. Perspective, see?"

"Whatever," I mumbled. "But she broke up with you because of it?"

"Not right away." His voice turned soft again. "She actually stuck by me through a lot of the hardest parts, which I'm grateful for. But in the end... she decided a life with me was not the best thing for her."

"That's a very nice way of speaking about someone who dumped you. After agreeing to marry you, no less!" My words came out harshly while a storm of emotions churned in my stomach. Anger and jealousy at a woman I never met? Oh, they were all brewing in there.

Connor shrugged, appearing utterly unfazed. "She didn't sign up for a life with a double amputee. Of course, it killed me at the time, but it's been years now. I don't fault her for wanting an easier life."

"I do," I huffed. "If she loved you, she would have stayed with you, no matter what. You don't just abandon someone you make a commitment to."

"It wasn't just the legs, babe," he said. "My PTSD was bad right after coming back. I was a completely different person than before. I pushed her away and upset her a lot. So some of the blame rests on me, too."

"You couldn't help any of that happening," I protested. "You didn't choose to lose your legs or have PTSD."

"True," he replied. "But shit happens sometimes. And sometimes it affects the people close to you, and they have to do what's right for themselves. Like you running away."

I lifted my head up to look at him. "What do you mean?"

"You did that to protect yourself after giving so much to those around you for so long."

"You're right," I admitted. "But I still want to go back at some point to help my younger siblings. They all deserve better than that hellhole."

"You will." He closed his hand around my fingers and brought them to his lips. "I mean, you're hellbent on saving *everyone,* so I'm sure you will." I felt his smile against my knuckles.

"Yeah, I can't seem to help it."

I looked over his body to the wolf family still huddled up and breathing quietly on the floor. The father had curled up into a semicircle of brilliant white fur, standing out like a ghost in the darkness. He laid like a dog would, with his jaw resting on the ground and his paw-like hands on either side of his face. His pups clung to his side, burying themselves in his fur.

"What's your next step for them?" Connor asked.

"I don't know," I answered. My entire focus had been getting them out of there. Now that we succeeded? I had no clue. "I guess rest for the night, figure out food in the morning, then see if we can communicate if they need anything else. Maybe they have a pack or something, I don't know." I returned my gaze to Connor. "Are you still worried about them hurting us?"

"No," he said. "You were right. There's something... really human about them."

"The kids stopped fighting me once I told them we were helping," I said. "I think letting them be near their dad shows we're not planning on using them again."

"So we figure it out in the morning, then," Connor mumbled sleepily. He was already drifting off.

I only realized then how tired I was, too. The adrenaline rush of our rescue mission drained everything out of me.

Connor flipped onto his side, drawing me against him as the little spoon. He dropped a kiss to my neck and curled around me with a contented sigh. I never went to sleep so deeply before, nor feeling so protected.

19

MELODY

I woke up to dappled sunlight streaming through the windows. I blinked, rubbed my eyes, rolled over, and stretched. Connor laid shirtless next to me, the sight of him making me instantly more awake.

How was it that this big, intimidating guy looked so cute when he slept? His brows pinched gently, full lips slightly parted, and the hypnotic rise and fall of his chest brought a lazy smile to my face. Especially after everything he told me last night, my body tingled in places I once wanted no one to touch. But the sight of him that morning awakened an ache deep in my core.

I leaned over him to check on our new companions on the floor. I leaned so far, unable to believe my eyes that I careened right over Connor's body and onto the floor.

"Connor!" I shouted. "Wake up, they're gone!"

"Hrm?" he mumbled groggily as I shoved open the trailer door. Sure enough, it was unlocked.

I stumbled outside, my eyes blinking as they adjusted to the morning sunlight.

Connor parked us in a small clearing of forest that resembled a campsite. I spun around in a circle, taking in the fresh, earthy scent in the air, the tall pine trees filtering out the sun, and the complete lack of human, wolf, or any other living soul.

In disbelief, I walked around the trailer, but only more trees and dense forest surrounded us.

"They're gone, babe." Connor sat on the edge of the bed wearing only his boxers as he looked out the open trailer door.

"But why?" I tore my fingers through my bird's nest of hair.

"Dad probably thought it was best," he mused. "We got them out of there, but they still don't know us. He was probably willing to risk living out in the woods rather than let someone hurt his kids again."

"I guess..." I chewed my lip. My mind thirsted for knowledge about these wolf people. I had so many questions that would now go unanswered.

"Come back in, Mel," Connor said. "Let's get some breakfast in us and figure out what the hell we're doing with ourselves."

After taking another long look through the trees and listening intently, I reluctantly obliged.

Connor sat at the small table to prepare breakfast, then hoisted himself up to sit on the counter to throw everything into a skillet. I heated up tortillas in the microwave, and within minutes we had ourselves some breakfast fajitas.

"You're still thinking about them," he observed once we finished our silent meal.

"I mean, aren't you curious?" I asked. "What are they?

Where did they come from? Are there more of them out there? A few hundred people saw them. Why isn't this on the news?"

"Mel, of course they're just as real as you and I. We both know that." Connor wiped his mouth on a napkin. "But the rest of the world would probably write them off as a hoax, which is a good thing. If you think the ring-master was a sadistic fuck, imagine what'll happen if the government gets ahold of them?"

"But I don't want to do anything like that," I protested. "I want to learn about them, help them more if they need it. I'm just so fascinated. They're intelligent, Connor! They responded like humans would."

"I know you wouldn't hurt a fly, babe," he smiled. "But like I said, they don't know they can trust you. If they're intelligent as you say, Dad wanted to do the best thing for his kids, so he made a choice."

"You're right. I know that," I groaned. "I just feel like this was a once-in-a-lifetime opportunity, to meet an intelligent species that isn't human."

"Who knows? Maybe you'll get abducted by aliens, too," Connor joked and laughed at my ensuing glare. "In all seriousness, though, you saved their lives, babe." He reached across the table for my hand and his gaze dropped shyly. "Not only do you have a heart of gold, you're brave and you're strong. Not many people are like that."

I dropped my own gaze, unsure how to handle such glowing compliments from a guy I increasingly found myself crushing on. My mind raced at how to respond and came up with nothing. Before Connor, no one had ever been good to me, as in genuinely kind and not just nice to me when they wanted something.

And just as quickly as it began, the moment was over.

"So," Connor released my hand, leaned back, and stretched his arms above his head. "What's next for us, babe?"

My heart skipped a beat. Was he referring to *us* or...?

"What do you mean?"

He gave me a funny look. "I mean in terms of money. The next job. Our food and gas aren't gonna last forever."

"Oh, right." My face heated, betraying me as I tried to play it cool. "Um, I'm not sure. What do you suggest?"

"Well, I've got two skills at this point. The main one being stilt acrobatics. I'd rather not do it forever, but the easiest way for me to get fast, legal money is to join another carnival."

"Makes sense," I nodded. "What's your other skill?"

"You might find that out later," he said with a wolfish grin.

The warmth in my cheeks flared up into a blazing inferno throughout my whole body. Heat pooled in my center like a fiery lake. The more time I spent with him, the more I wanted to let go, to let him in.

"But only if or when you want to," he added with a wink. "What about you, Mel? What are your vocational skills?"

"I don't really have any," I admitted. "I never could get a job during school because I had to take care of my siblings. This stint with the carnival has been the only job I've ever had."

"So looks like it's back to the ol' freak show for both of us," he mused, taking a sip of coffee.

"I really don't mind it," I piped up. "Aside from, you know, Syko, I actually had fun performing. If there's a traveling show out there that isn't abusive to its performers, I'd be happy staying in this business."

"Heh," Connor scoffed. "They may not be Syko but trust me, babe. All of them have some level of corruption and dirty business practices. It's kind of like pimping. When you're profiting off of human bodies, you're not usually too concerned with the ethics of the situation."

"Well, maybe we can start our own carnival," I joked. "Where everyone is treated fairly, and it's not a meat market."

Connor nearly choked on his coffee. "Ah, to be eighteen and full of dreams again," he laughed.

"Don't make fun of me, old man!" I threw my last hunk of tortilla at him, prompting him to reach around the table and tickle my waist.

After a few minutes of playful tickle-wrestling and stealing kisses in between, we got cleaned up and got ready to find work. Connor said he knew another carnival manager in a small town about two hours away, so off we went.

It was a long, slow, lumbering drive through a windy forest road. I kept looking out the passenger window, still hoping to see flashes of white fur through the trees and brush. But I eventually fell asleep with my cheek against the glass until Connor shook my shoulder gently.

"We're here, sleeping beauty," he said with a nuzzle and kiss to my neck.

I followed him out, quickly realizing we were in an RV park still surrounded by forest. But over the treeline stood a slowly moving Ferris wheel. Past the trailers and through the trees, I caught glimpses of brightly colored tents and booths being set up.

"What town is this?" I asked.

"Crying Falls, Mississippi," Connor answered as we approached a simple wooden building, the only permanent structure on the grounds. It looked to be an office or general store. "Population five-hundred-eighty in the winter and quadruple that during summer carnival season."

My stomach did a flip-flop. "A lot of people come to this one, huh?"

"Yeah, it becomes some weird hybrid between traveling carnival, Burning Man, and music festival. The sideshow scene is pretty big here."

"Sideshow?"

Connor grabbed my hand and pulled me close. "That's us, babe," he chuckled, with a kiss to the top of my head. "The freaks."

The carnival manager was a thin, reedy man who recognized Connor instantly. He pretty much ignored me, which I was honestly happy about. Any opportunity I took to not show off my cleavage to beg for a job, I happily took.

"Are you two an act together?" asked Nigel, the manager who seemed to notice me for the first time.

"Yes," Connor answered quickly, with a hint of growl in his voice. His grip on my hand grew firm and possessive.

"Wonderful," Nigel beamed. "I'll show you through the grounds, then we can get you on a schedule."

The carnival grounds were much more expansive than the one in Drowningville and seemed to have a lot more to offer. Vendors and craftspeople were setting up their booths for the coming visitors. The usual carnival games, rides, and food carts were being set up as well. A large stage for music was at the far end, hula hoopers practiced their routine in a nearby field, and the massive Ferris wheel looked over it all like an omniscient eye. It really felt more like a festival than a carnival.

Connor and I got some fresh tacos and ears of corn from a local vendor after our tour, then set up a campfire back at our trailer. Already the sky began turning pink then purple with the setting sun, and more campfires illuminated in the darkness. I didn't realize getting here and checking the place out took most of the day.

"Beer, babe?" Connor held a bottle out to me as we settled next to our fire.

"No, thanks," I answered.

"What, not a party girl?" he teased.

"Not really."

I became deeply preoccupied with roasting my marshmallow and he thankfully left it alone. I didn't want to get into explaining my alcoholic mother and the string of men just like her that came in and out of our house. If Connor could have his secrets, so could I.

Sitting together by the fire, I watched his beer intake with nervous apprehension. People drinking always made me guarded. Dealing with Syko didn't ease my nerves in the slightest.

Alcohol brought out the worst in people, as far as I was concerned. And here was someone I was starting to care about. Could he feel the tense shield surrounding me as he cracked open a second bottle?

To my relief, Connor stopped at two. He eased back in his lawn chair, staring at the flames with the same hot but scowling expression he always wore.

"What's our act gonna be?" I asked. "Same as the one in Drowningville?"

"No idea." He never looked up from the flames. "We'll figure something out tomorrow."

I left it at that. He didn't seem to be in the mood to talk.

Despite the sugar rush from my s'mores, I soon felt my eyelids drooping. Looking over at Connor, I saw he was nodding off as well. The fire went down to embers and the darkness creeped in all around us.

"Hey." I leaned over and rubbed the back of his neck. "Ready to call it a night?"

He nodded, bringing our stuff inside while I covered the fire with water and dirt from the ground. After following him in and washing my hands, I noticed him grimacing as he slid his prosthetics off. The skin just below his knee was red and tender.

"You okay?"

"I'll be alright," he said gruffly. "Just a long day of driving and walking puts pressure on the ol' stubs."

"Here." I rummaged through my backpack until I found the small sample bottle of lotion I got from the homeless shelter.

His protests turned to pleasant sighs as I rubbed it in all around where his legs ended. Just as I figured, the skin was dry and cracked. My fingers worked deeply into the tissue around his knees to bring circulation back to the area.

"Thanks, babe," he muttered softly.

"Of course." I slid my palms up his powerful quads and tilted my chin up for a kiss.

His mouth caught mine so sweetly and so hungrily. A moan escaped his mouth as he cupped the back of my head to deepen the kiss. Our tongues clashed and danced with a heightened passion and more intensity than ever before. My skin felt alive, like the living, breathing organ it was, and it wanted more of Connor. So much more.

But ever the gentleman, he slowly, reluctantly pulled away. My body responded before my brain could catch up. I climbed into his lap, straddling his thighs, and rested my aching core over the hardening bulge in his pants. He let out a small groan of surprise as my arms wrapped around his shoulders, my chest pressed to his, and my tongue surged into his mouth for more of him.

"Mel," he rasped when our mouths broke apart. "Are you sure...?"

The question seemed to break a spell over me and I withdrew just slightly, my self-consciousness taking a front seat to my body's desires.

"I don't know," I stammered as I pulled away. "Kind of, but maybe not all the way... Shit, I'm sorry."

He caught my waist and pulled me back for another kiss before I could slide completely off his lap. Kisses peppered my face and neck as his hands slid up my back, holding me in an embrace that was just as reassuring as it was possessive. Together, we leaned over until we collapsed on the mattress. His kisses continued, and I writhed against him as his hands grew more adventurous.

"Grab my hands if you want me to stop, or just tell me," he murmured, nipping the side of my neck before his mouth traveled lower. "I just want you to relax and feel good, babe."

My nerves slowly melted away as he took his time with me, kissing and caressing until my legs parted, eager to release the heat and coiled up tension building inside of me. Lifting my shirt, his hands and lips traveled across my waist, belly, and hips in a sensual, hypnotizing pattern until I couldn't stand it anymore. I took his hands and placed them on my breasts.

Growing bolder, his hands slid under my bra cups to be quickly joined by his mouth. His tongue swirled around my nipples and flicked against the stiff peaks. It felt so good, I didn't even realize my hips were lifting off the bed to press against him. He kissed the valley between my breasts as his fingertips traveled down to tease the sensitive skin of my inner thighs until I trembled.

His palm splayed against my belly, it dipped lower and lower until he was inside my shorts. My hips bucked when he reached my core. I was too wound up, too fucking turned on to be self-conscious of my wetness that now coated his hand.

"Oh my god, Mel," he groaned and kissed me savagely as if my pleasure was his own.

Once he found my clit, it was over. I clawed at his back and bucked against his hand, my pleasure climbing higher than I ever thought possible. He pressed in hard, fast circles that showed he knew exactly what he was doing. He took my nipple between his teeth and that's when I came apart. His hot palm cupped my vulva, watching me in fascination as I rode the waves of my orgasm. Lost in the jolts shooting throughout my entire body, I forgot all about staying guarded and self-conscious.

When my orgasm subsided into warmth and relaxation, Connor kissed me one final time before dropping behind me. He curled around me and pulled me against him with an arm around my waist. Our usual spooning position, but where it felt somewhat platonic before, there was a new feeling of intimacy now.

I flipped over to face him, running my hand along his neck and jaw in the darkness.

"Do you want me to, um..."

"No, babe." He kissed the tip of my nose. "All I wanted was for you to relax and feel good. Did it work?"

I giggled and found his mouth with mine. "Yes. That felt amazing."

"Good. Don't worry about me, Mel. I've gone years without. It's more important that you can relax and trust me." He grew quiet for a moment. "I know what it's like to feel like no one is decent or trustworthy. I'm willing to prove that I'm not going to hurt you, babe."

If that orgasm left me blissfully empty, raw emotion now filled that space inside me. I was stunned, moved beyond words, but a small voice whispered a reminder that I'd fallen for pretty words before.

So I just kissed him and whispered, "Thank you. Goodnight."

He mumbled a goodnight as I flipped over again, curling my back against his chest and allowing sleep to settle into my relaxed, sated body.

I *wanted* to trust him. I wanted to believe he was the first good, genuine person I met. But every person I was supposed to trust ended in heartache. My mom. My older sister. Teachers. Counselors. Ex-boyfriends. Time after time, their actions toward me proved I was better off protecting myself than allowing someone else to protect me. Because without fail, they threw me to the wolves every time I let my guard down.

I wanted to believe Connor was different. We had common ground in being guarded and untrusting of others for good reasons. My heart and my body practically begged me to give themselves to him. But time would tell, especially if we continued doing this carnival thing together. If this business was as seedy and corrupt as he said, it would certainly test whatever this was between us. If this was a convincing act like all the others were, his true colors would come out eventually.

And if they did, I had to make sure my heart wasn't already in his hands when that time came.

Just before I drifted off in his arms, I swore I heard a wolf howling in the distance.

⁂

THANK you so much for reading *Freak Show*! Book 2 in the series, *Abra Cadabra, is available now!*

⁂

OR IF YOU'D rather grab the whole series in one go, the **Harem of Freaks boxed set is available here!**

NEWSLETTER & READER GROUP

Never miss a book release, plus get three *free* short stories when you sign up for my newsletter!

Grab your freebies at:
crystalashbooks.com/freebies

You can also join my reader group on Facebook to get updates and hang out with fellow readers.

Join Crystal's Coven at:
facebook.com/groups/crystalscoven

ABOUT THE AUTHOR

Crystal Ash is a USA Today Bestselling Author from California. She loves writing steamy, heart-wrenching romance with tortured heroes, especially if they're in a reverse harem. Crystal's other loves include animals, mythology, and well-crafted alcohol, most of which can also be found in her stories.

When she's not writing, she's probably drinking craft beer with her husband or trying to coax her feral cat into accepting affection.

crystalashbooks.com

facebook.com/Crystal.Ash.Romance

instagram.com/crystalashbooks

amazon.com/author/crystalash

bookbub.com/profile/crystal-ash